THE FORBIDDEN LOVE OF THE OLD BOOK

ARNAV HERLEKAR

Contents

I

A Story of Spaces in Between

Under the dark sky, the air was heavy with the scent of sweat, dust, and devotion. The monsoon clouds had not yet burst, but they loomed, low and threatening, as if holding their breath along with the city. Mumbai was a living, breathing entity tonight — its heartbeat drummed into the streets, echoing from the chawls and concrete towers alike. The Dahi Handi festival had taken over.

The chants were relentless.

"Govinda aala re aala!"

The words rose from a thousand throats and curled into the night like sacred smoke. Men in saffron headbands pushed through crowds, women watched from balconies with plates of aarti, and children darted between feet, chasing toy flutes and half-melted kulfis.

There was joy in the air, yes. But beneath it, like a second rhythm, was something rawer. Hunger. Desperation. Faith.

And at the center of this pulsing madness stood the handi.

It hung high above the street, swaying gently in the monsoon breeze. Butter, curd, flowers, and coins, with a piece of peacock feather—all nestled inside, daring someone to reach it. The human pyramid was already forming below, muscle on muscle, heart on heart, sweat bonding strangers into fleeting unity.

At the top of it was her.

Radhika.

She wasn't supposed to be there. Tradition had its rules. Unspoken, yet deeply embedded. But Radhika was a quiet rebellion wrapped in grace. Her presence at the top was no accident—it was a decision. A declaration.

She climbed like a story being rewritten. Every step she took was a word crossed out from the old scripts of who gets to rise and who stays below. Her palms pressed onto bare backs, her feet gripped shoulders, and her eyes never wavered from the earthen pot above. Her dupatta flapped like a forgotten prayer, her braid whipped behind her like a tale untamed.

And in the crowd, half-hidden beneath the shadow of a half-fallen banner, stood Anay.

He had not planned to be here.

That morning, he told himself he wouldn't come. That he had let go. That he didn't need to see her anymore. But pain is a magnet — subtle and cruel — and some wounds crave proximity.

His eyes found her before his mind was ready.

There she was — rising, lit by halogen lights and the faith of everyone below her. Radhika. The same woman who once wore yellow just because he said it reminded him of summer. The same girl who danced barefoot in their kitchen to old Hindi songs, flour in her hair, laughter in her teeth. The same soul who once held his hand in temple queues and talked about forever like it was a place they'd surely visit.

And yet, tonight, she was someone else too.

Untouchable. Distant. Someone whose story no longer belonged to him.

Anay stood still as the crowd surged and screamed around him. Firecrackers burst overhead, but he didn't flinch. He watched her, eyes tracing every fragile second of her climb.

And for one heartbeat — just one — she looked down.

Did she see him?

He didn't know. But something flickered across her face. A twitch at the corner of her lips. A pause.

Then the pyramid trembled.

Someone slipped.

A gasp sliced through the chant.

And Radhika fell.

She didn't fall like in the movies. There was no slow-motion. No violin swell. Just gravity, cruel and swift. Her body twisted mid-air, her arms reaching instinctively — for something, anything — and then hitting the street with a crack that even the drums couldn't drown.

The world reacted before Anay did.

People screamed. Ran. Formed a ring around her. Someone shouted for water. Someone else for space. A young man in a blue shirt bent over her, touching her face with panicked familiarity. Anay saw it all.

And yet, he didn't move.

His hands were fists in his pockets. His jaw clenched. And his chest — that fragile prison — ached with the kind of pain that had no name. He watched her, motionless, like a man witnessing the collapse of a temple he used to pray in.

And then he smiled.

It wasn't joy.

It was survival.

A crooked, bitter thing that sat on his face like an old scar. The kind of smile a man wears when he's tired of breaking himself to save someone who doesn't want to be saved by him.

He turned.

And he walked away.

Two lanes over, away from the crowd's roar, the street was quieter — the aftermath of devotion lingering in marigold petals and muddy puddles. Kabir waited on the hood of Anay's car, bottle of water in hand, tapping it rhythmically against his knee.

When he saw Anay, he stood up, eyes narrowing.

"You saw her fall," he said, no greeting, just the truth.

Anay didn't stop walking. "You said you wanted to talk."

Kabir stepped in his path. "You saw Radhika fall from a goddamn pyramid and you're just—what? Taking a stroll?"

Anay pulled a cigarette from behind his ear, lit it with hands that shook more than he let on. The first drag was deep, like he was trying to drown something inside.

"She's your wife, Anay."

"She was," Anay corrected.

Kabir's voice lowered. "Don't do that. Don't play in the cold. I know you. You still love her."

"I never said I didn't."

"Then why the hell didn't you go to her?"

Anay looked up at the sky, as if the answer might be written in the clouds, or hidden behind the stars they used to wish on. His eyes fell to a boy across the street, chasing a red balloon down the gutter.

He exhaled slowly.

"Because I've spent years loving her in ways that ruined me," he said, his voice barely audible. "And today... I just wanted to watch her fall without breaking myself to catch her again."

Kabir was silent.

Because what does one say to a man who loves so deeply that it hurts him just to breathe in the same air? What words can soften the edges of a heart that's been sanded down to nothing?

Anay flicked the ash off his cigarette. The ember glowed briefly, then died.

"You wanted to know why I came. Why didn't I stay? Why did I let her fall?"

He looked Kabir in the eyes now — not cold, but tired. So damn tired.

"Let me tell you a story."

And so, under flickering streetlights and memory's burden, the past began to unspool — a love once divine, now broken, and still somehow alive.

II

THE VOW IN SILENCE

Before heartbreak and silence, before words were weapons and time a thief, there was a boy — barely taller than his schoolbag — who saw a girl on a rainy day and never quite recovered from it.

Anay was ten.

It was the kind of July morning when the clouds hung low, swollen with secrets, and the rain refused to stop. It wasn't a gentle drizzle — it poured like the sky had remembered something sorrowful.

Everything was soaked: roads, notebooks, socks, and voices. The school looked like an island, its corridors echoing with soggy footsteps and children's laughter.

Anay stood alone under the rusted canopy near the library, biting the inside of his cheek and watching the playground flood. His shirt stuck to his back. His shoes squelched. But he didn't care.

Because she was there. Radhika.

She wasn't like the other girls, and Anay didn't mean that in the silly, romanticized way stories often describe the beginnings of young love. She was simply... different. Real in a way that demanded your attention and delicate in a way that made you afraid to breathe too hard around her.

That day, she was barefoot, hopping through puddles in the back courtyard. Her hair clung to her temples, wild and messy, her laughter scattering the air like monsoon birds. Her skirt had risen to her knees, revealing scratched shins and muddy toes. She didn't care. She was alive in the way children are before the world tells them to shrink.

And Anay... he watched.

Something bloomed inside him — not like fire, not even like thunder. It was quieter than that. Like ink slowly soaking into paper, staining him forever.

She didn't notice him. Not then, not ever.

But from that moment onward, Anay noticed everything about her.

They lived on the same street — not close enough to be friends, but close enough for fate to tease him. He learned, over time, the rhythm of her life: when she left for school, when she returned, the melody she hummed when she watered the plants in her balcony garden. His room was opposite hers, just high enough to see her house. In the early evenings, when the sun poured gold through the dusty windows, he would sit at his desk pretending to do homework, while his eyes followed her silhouette behind those ivory lace curtains.

Radhika's room was a story in itself. There were windchimes — old-fashioned ones. Tiny brass bells, seashell strands, colored glass, wooden carvings — all catching light and air like whispered secrets. Every time they rang, it was like they were calling to him. Telling him: she's home. She's safe. She's near.

Sometimes, late at night, when the city was done talking and even the stars seemed to sigh, he would hear her softly strumming an old guitar. She wasn't great at it — often pausing mid-chord to mumble lyrics or hum tunes off-key. But Anay listened like it was the only music that mattered. He'd lie in bed, hands behind his head, pretending the song was for him.

He memorized her presence the way others memorized holy verses. He noticed how she twirled her pen between her fingers when she was thinking. How she always bit her straw before taking a sip. How she talked to her dog like it was a little brother. How she lingered a little longer under the lamp post outside her house, bathing in the soft amber light as if it were starlight just meant for her.

Anay fell for her in fragments.

In tiny, stolen glimpses and soft collisions of fate. He fell for her when she lent her umbrella to an old woman and walked home in the rain. He fell for her when she helped a younger kid tie his shoelaces without being asked. He fell for her when she cried during the Independence Day speech because the soldier's letter reminded her of her father who had passed away too young.

His love was old-school. The kind of love that didn't need attention. That didn't need photographs or proof. It sat quietly in the corners of his heart, like a lamp kept lit on a windowsill for someone who might never come home.

He never imagined walking up to her, never imagined saying it aloud. That wasn't the point.

He just... loved her.

He made her his North Star. He crafted every dream and every version of himself with her in mind. He woke up before dawn to train. He studied with quiet intensity. He became the strongest in his class, not to impress her, but to feel worthy of her in the secret world he built around her.

He wanted to become a man she could lean on — not because she asked, but because he would always be standing behind her, unseen but solid. A shadow that protected her. A silence that promised.

Some evenings, when he was sure she wouldn't notice, he'd write her letters — not to send, but to keep. He kept them folded inside an old shoebox beneath his bed, alongside dried flowers he picked on his way home, movie tickets he imagined watching with her someday, and other silly memorabilia that didn't matter to the world but meant everything to him.

And Radhika? She never really saw him. She knew him in passing. A familiar boy. A face you recognize in a crowd but never really turn toward. A neighbor. A classmate. Someone who once helped carry chairs at a school event. The boy who always let others go first.

And Anay accepted that.

He didn't love her to be loved back. His love wasn't transactional. It was more like a promise he made to himself. A vow without an altar. A song hummed with no audience.

He remembered once, years later, standing on his balcony while she laughed on hers, talking to a boy he didn't recognize. She looked radiant — the way joy made her unaware of her beauty. He felt a sharp ache.

Not jealousy. No. It was the ache of watching an old letter burn — one you never sent, but read every night.

Still, he didn't stop loving her.

She was the background music of his life — always there, soft and essential. And if no one else ever knew that, it was okay.

He didn't need the world to understand.

He didn't even need her to understand.

He had made a decision long ago.

To be the man who stood quietly, even when unnoticed.

To be the boy who loved gently, even without return.

To choose her, endlessly.

And that was enough.

For a while.

Until the day he realized love, too, could feel like a burden when it had no place to land.

But even then — even when everything else cracked and bled — he still carried her in the parts of him that no one else ever got to see.

The boy who loved her? He never really left. He just learned to stay quiet, the way old promises do.

III
PORCHLIGHT DAYS

The first time Anay Lele ever spoke to Radhika Joshi, it wasn't beneath fairy lights or in a café with indie music playing. It was in a sun-drenched college corridor that smelled of glue guns, acrylic paint, and ambition. The college was gearing up for the annual inter-college fest, and the auditorium was a scene of beautiful chaos. People rushed about with wires, banners, scripts, and props, trying to stitch together an evening of glamour and applause.

Radhika stood in the middle of it all like she belonged to a different world. Not because she sought attention, but because she didn't. Her dupatta was loosely draped, one end caught in the breeze, clipboard clutched in her hand like it was a shield. Her eyes flitted from prop to prop, person to person, focused and slightly withdrawn — a girl who had learned how to thrive without being loud.

She was speaking to someone on the phone, her voice quiet but assertive. You could tell she didn't enjoy speaking to crowds, but when she had to, she did it with grace — like someone who'd practiced leadership in front of her bedroom mirror.

"You — can you help me find someone from logistics?" she asked, turning abruptly and pointing at Anay.

He had been standing by the pillar, half-invisible like always, holding a box of fairy lights. The words hit him with the softness of a love letter and the force of a windstorm.

He blinked. "Uh, yeah... I think the logistics guy's name is Ronit. I saw him near the back entrance."

"Great. Can you tell him to get the black curtain backdrop up in ten minutes? We're out of time," she said without missing a beat, already turning back.

He nodded, turned, and jogged off. His heart beat loud in his chest. For her, it was another instruction. For him, it was history. It was the first page of a book he'd unknowingly been writing in his head for years.

The college was old, built during the post-independence architectural phase — a mix of British colonial balconies and Maharashtrian stone arches. There were banyan trees older than the professors, corridors echoing with laughter, secrets, and generations of love stories whispered through hostel windows.

Radhika, with her quiet brilliance, was like a walking contradiction. Reserved but competent. Shy but capable.

She didn't socialize much outside of her work; she ate her lunch alone on the third step of the amphitheatre, with a book in one hand and earphones in the other.

Anay had seen her there too — smiling to herself at something she read, or scribbling in her journal like she was stitching thoughts she never meant to share.

Anay, in contrast, preferred the shadows — behind the lights, managing wires, perfecting the audio. He liked being invisible. Until she saw him.

The second time they met, it was in the library.

She dropped a thick book — *Modern Urban Design Principles* — right beside his laptop. He looked up, startled.

"Sorry," she said softly. "Didn't mean to startle you."

He shook his head. "No, no. You didn't."

She sat across the table, and for a whole hour, both pretended to study. He didn't speak, didn't even glance directly. But every click of her pen, every time she flipped a page — it stayed with him.

What Radhika didn't know was that Anay had seen her long before she saw him. From his room window on the third floor of their bungalow, he had a clear view of a bungalow diagonally opposite. It was Joshi's residence.

He had often seen her reading by the window, headphones in, lost to the world. Sometimes sketching. Sometimes laughing with someone on the phone.

Once, she danced alone in her room — a twirl, a skip, the kind only meant for joy.

He never starred. He observed. Like a painter watches light fall on a sculpture. Quietly. Respectfully. Reverently.

She was a world he could never touch but one he'd quietly memorized.

Both families had unknowingly circled the same spaces.

The Lele family was dignified — understated in their wealth, rich in their values. Shirish Lele, Anay's father, was a man of few but wise words, known for his business ethics in the infrastructure consultancy field. He had raised Anay on discipline, Marathi poetry, and stories of building bridges — literal and emotional.

The Joshis were more expressive — celebrated in architecture circles, known for designing homes with heart. Radhika's mother, Seema, designed interiors with a touch of nostalgia. Her father, Rajan, was often called the mad genius, sketching layouts on restaurant napkins and temple receipts.

They attended the same Ganpati Mandals. Their names appeared together in Marathi matrimony magazines. But the children never crossed paths — not until college.

Over the next few months, Anay and Radhika had a dozen near-conversations. She thanked him once for fixing a mic before her speech. He offered her an umbrella one day during a surprise downpour. She borrowed his pen during a group meeting. Tiny things.

He never tried to flirt. He never confessed. He just... watched. And felt.

He began carrying an extra pen, just in case. He'd sit closer during fest meetings. Not next to her. Just close enough.

It was old-school love — quiet, clean, sacred. The kind that doesn't ask for anything, yet gives everything.

One Sunday evening, Anay was sitting on the balcony beside his father. They shared silence like old friends. The breeze carried the smell of rain-soaked earth and jasmine from a nearby vendor.

Mr. Lele folded his newspaper and sipped his coffee. "You remember that firm from Pune — Joshi & Daughters?"

Anay stiffened slightly. "Yeah, I've heard of them."

"We're entering a joint venture with them. Township development in Navi Mumbai. Brilliant family. Talented daughter, I hear. Went to your college, I think."

Anay didn't respond. Just watched a kite dancing in the orange sky.

Radhika Joshi.

Her name in his father's mouth felt like the universe had dropped a breadcrumb.

He smiled faintly, sipping his tea.

Sometimes fate doesn't crash and doors open. Sometimes it just sat beside you with a cup of tea and whispered, *it's time.*

And for Anay Lele, everything — her voice, her laugh, the way she looked when she spoke to the sky — had always felt like the beginning of something inexplicably his.

And this time, the world was finally starting to agree.

It had been weeks since the inter-college fest, and the air between Radhika and Anay had shifted, almost imperceptibly — like the season changing between two breaths. Where once there had only been glances and passing moments, now there were occasional interactions. Still short, still shy, but real. And even more than that, there were shared silences — the kind that only two people who begin to recognize each other can sit in without feeling awkward.

Their connection wasn't loud or dramatic. It didn't thrive on texts or midnight calls. It existed in the soft brush of shoulders in the college corridor, in the way Anay started carrying an extra bottle of water during fest practices because Radhika always forgot hers. But she never took it. Not once. She would politely decline or act like she didn't notice. And she never saved him a seat. She simply went about her day — quiet, focused, introverted — and if Anay happened to sit near her, it was a coincidence. Nothing more.

They weren't close — not friends, not even familiar — but there was a rhythm beginning to form, a recognition.

At least from Anay's side. Radhika remained distant, a little reserved, her world neatly tucked behind unread books and silent thoughts.

Outside the college walls, a separate bond was taking root — not between them, but between their families.

The Lele family — Anay's family — was the kind of well-bred, old-money household where class met humility. Their sprawling bungalow in Shivaji Park was an elegant blend of teakwood furniture, ivory-toned curtains, book-lined walls, and quiet music that lingered in the background like a memory. Every corner smelled of tradition — sandalwood, filter coffee, freshly pressed linen.

Amruta Lele, Anay's mother, was a graceful woman who rarely raised her voice but carried an aura that silenced rooms. A lover of Carnatic music and quiet temple mornings, she brought balance to their spirited household. Isha, Anay's younger sister, was the dramatic artist in the family — dressed in oversized hoodies and oversized opinions, she painted walls, staged performances in the drawing room, and recited poetry with the intensity of a thunderstorm.

But it was Shirish Lele, the patriarch, who was the anchor. A retired architect, now consultant, Shirish was the kind of man who wore handwoven kurtas and used fountain pens. He had a sharp intellect, a sharper sense of humor, and a deeply rooted belief in the idea of kindness. He treated his children like adults and his employees like family. He was Anay's role model, more through his actions than his words.

Anay and Shirish had the kind of bond that didn't need to be advertised in hugs or loud laughter. It was a quiet companionship — made up of shared silences on the porch, debates over old architecture books, teasing banter about Anay's stubbornness, and moments when Shirish would quietly leave Anay's favorite filter coffee by his study desk during exams. They spoke less and understood more.

There was an unspoken pride in Shirish's eyes every time he looked at Anay — pride not in his grades or achievements, but in his empathy, in the gentleness he carried even while trying to be strong. And Anay, for all his aloofness in college and confidence among friends, always found himself softening around his father. Because Shirish was not just his parent — he was the quiet compass that never forced a direction but always pointed home.

The Joshi family, on the other hand, was quieter in comparison but similar in essence. Their home was filled with earthy tones, floor plants, and meticulously designed interiors — courtesy of Rajan Joshi, Radhika's father, an architect who saw design in everything, even how the spoons were placed in the drawer.

Seema Joshi, Radhika's mother, was warm-hearted and conservative in a gentle, endearing way. She worried about what society would think, double-checked every door before sleeping, and still made Radhika wear black thread around her wrist. She made perfect theplas and read spiritual books before bed. She adored Radhika but often misunderstood the silences she carried.

When the two families met — officially — it was over a casual business dinner at the Lele bungalow.

Shirish had extended the invite to discuss a new venture: a joint architectural and development project — a sustainable luxury township just beyond Navi Mumbai. The Joshi firm was to co-lead the design, while the Lele group would helm the execution and investment.

Radhika, who was clueless about the invite until the last moment, found herself at the familiar porch of Anay's home — only this time, it wasn't him she was meeting at college or in passing. This was *his* world, his people.

The dinner was unexpectedly comfortable. Rajan and Shirish immediately clicked — both being architects with bold ideas and soft hearts. Amruta and Seema shared a quiet bond, discussing everything from devotional music to interior lighting. Isha and Radhika ended up laughing over a shared dislike for a professor they both knew.

The evening stretched into night with laughter, warmth, and moments that blurred the line between professional and personal. But even so, Radhika and Anay remained reserved with each other — polite, observant, and distant in their own ways. There was no flirtation, no familiarity beyond what was courteous and familial.

Later that evening, as the house quieted, Anay found himself on the veranda swing with his father.

Shirish took a sip of coffee, eyes twinkling with teasing mischief. "That Joshi girl... spark in her eyes. Cute, no?"

Anay nearly choked. "Baba... come on."

"What? I'm old, not blind," Shirish chuckled. "I'm just saying, these coincidences... It's like the universe decided to give your dull life some drama. Maybe even a love story."

Anay rolled his eyes but smiled, unable to help it. The comment wasn't serious — just the kind of playful jab a father throws, nothing more. But beneath it, Anay could feel the warmth of being seen. It meant something that his father noticed — not in a pushy way, but in that gentle, knowing manner only Shirish could manage.

In the days that followed, Radhika and Anay saw more of each other — not just in college, but now at home too, when the families met for dinners, site visits, or weekend brunches. Their bond didn't deepen in words but in presence — consistent, quiet, familiar.

Anay began to thrive quietly in this growing proximity. His world felt lighter. He found himself smiling at nothing, making mental notes of things Radhika liked — filter coffee, sunflowers, soft instrumental music, the smell of wet earth.

Even Radhika, introverted and careful, started opening up in subtle ways. She would sometimes wait behind brunches to help Amruta with the dishes, or sit in Isha's room chatting about books. With Anay, she remained distant. Polite. Occasionally warm. But her walls stayed up.

Still, she intrigued him. She moved through the world like she didn't want to be seen — yet couldn't help but stand out.

But beneath all the sweetness, there was something else. Something no one could quite see.

Radhika had begun losing time.

Just tiny blips. Once, she forgot a line mid-conversation with Seema and claimed she was just tired. Another time, she paused on the balcony, staring at a point in the sky like she was listening to something only she could hear.

And once, Anay noticed her staring at the reflection of a tree in a glass door — her lips moving like she was having a conversation. When he asked her about it, she smiled, said, "Just thinking aloud," and walked away.

She often drew in her sketchbook — faceless men, distant landscapes, abstract patterns. But one particular drawing stood out to Anay when he caught a glimpse of it one afternoon: a boy, his back turned, standing under a banyan tree with birds flying overhead. There was something hauntingly beautiful about it. Radhika tore the page out before he could say anything.

"Just a dream," she murmured.

No one thought more of it.

Because what is a flicker in a world full of light?

And in the warm cocoon of two families bonding, two lives gently blooming into proximity, and a world that for once didn't demand explanations — Anay believed things were perfect. He didn't yet know that love sometimes hides in plain sight... and so does madness.

But for now, the verandas were full of laughter. The drawings stayed folded. And Radhika's world — and his — continued to bloom in a way that felt almost poetic.

Just like the beginning of a story they didn't yet know they were writing together.

IV
BENEATH THE STILLNESS

In their teens, they sat silently during a family lunch; now, they're seated again in the same garden, same chairs, just older, and the silence still speaks volumes.

Anay Lele looked up from his cup of black coffee. The mug had changed over the years—from steel to ceramic, his grip steadier, his shoulders broader—but Radhika was still the same. Maybe a little more grown into herself. A little more inward. But still, she held the air of someone halfway between a secret and a memory.

The garden at the Lele bungalow had aged gently with them. The bougainvillea vines now kissed the edge of the old wrought-iron gate. The swings still creaked when Isha, Anay's younger sister, dragged them into her late-night poetry readings, and the gravel path was slightly more worn. But everything else was as it had been ten years ago.

The chairs they sat on had hosted hundreds of conversations, none of which belonged to the two of them. Radhika and Anay were not talkers when it came to each other. Their connection was not built on what was spoken, but on what was held.

She sipped her tea, eyes following a butterfly hovering over a hibiscus flower. The mug in her hands was the same one she had always chosen—blue with a chipped rim. Her fingers rested on it delicately, as if even after all this time, she was afraid of holding things too tightly.

It wasn't awkward, this silence. It was just... familiar.

Their families, now old friends and business partners, had slipped into a rhythm of shared holidays, combined Ganpati celebrations, and the occasional weekend trip to Alibaug. It wasn't unusual for Anay and Radhika to end up in the same space.

But this—this quiet afternoon in the garden—felt different. Not because anything had changed between them, but because nothing had. And that, in a way, said everything.

Anay had grown into the man he once wanted to be. At 26, he had started handling core operations in the Lele-Joshi partnership project. His demeanor was still quietly confident, his words measured, and his presence calming. He was respected by the boardroom and adored by the site workers. He kept filter coffee sachets in his laptop bag and wore wooden-beaded bracelets his sister had made years ago. There was a steadiness in him, like an old song on loop.

Radhika, too, had carved her path. She now worked as a junior architect under her father, assisting in design models and creative curation. She preferred shadows to stage lights, perspectives to presentations. While she still drew in the back pages of her notebook, her real sketches now rested in blueprint folders and CAD drafts.

But her silence had deepened.

She often paused mid-sentence now, not because she didn't know what to say, but because she was lost in her own thought-scape. She would blink slowly, like returning from a world she alone could see. Once or twice, Seema had noticed her daughter humming a tune no one else recognized. But Seema assumed it was just an old bhajan stuck in her head.

Once, Shirish had seen her looking at a wall as though it would reply to her.

He didn't mention it.

It was during one of the weekly brunches that Anay noticed something.

Radhika was seated on the porch, sketchbook in hand. She was drawing a tree, but not any tree. It looked oddly familiar. He stepped closer.

"That looks like the banyan outside the farmhouse," he said casually.

She looked up, startled. Then smiled. "Does it?"

He nodded.

She turned the page before he could see the rest. A boy was half-drawn, back turned, standing beneath the tree.

"Just... something from imagination," she said lightly.

He didn't think much of it then.

But a few days later, when Isha mentioned how Radhika had been talking about the stars moving differently these days, he paused. It was said in jest, over chips and fizzy drinks. Isha, with her usual dramatic flair, had found it poetic. Anay laughed along. But something about it stuck with him.

Still, there was nothing unusual. Nothing that shouted for attention. No red flags. Just a gentle shift. Like the sky slightly dimming before twilight.

That evening, as dusk poured itself slowly across the veranda, the families gathered again for dinner.

The air was scented with sandalwood incense and freshly fried puris. Conversations floated between music, building permissions, and whether Alibaug had become too commercial.

Seema fussed over Radhika's plate. Amruta was teasing Shirish about his sudden obsession with terrariums. Rajan Joshi laughed easily, his usual guarded demeanor softened over dessert.

And Anay just watched.

Watched as his world moved gently around him. Watched Radhika laugh at something Isha whispered. Watched her fall silent again. Watched as she traced her fingers around the rim of her bowl, lost in thought.

He didn't know what he was feeling.

But something in him knew: whatever this was, it was going to stay with him for a long, long time.

Not because of what it was.

But because of what it wasn't.

The stillness between them was not empty.

It was waiting.

And maybe, in time, it would become something.

But for now, it was enough to sit side by side.

Same garden. Same chairs.

And a silence that knew everything.

But on the other half, The first time she whispered his name, it wasn't out loud.

It was in her mind, as she stood by the kitchen window, watching a leaf tumble down in slow spirals. There was no sound in the house except the hum of the refrigerator and a clock ticking like a soft heartbeat. Yet, she felt it—a presence.

Not physical. Not intrusive. Just... known.

A name floated in her thoughts like a soft chord, one she didn't remember learning but somehow knew by heart. It wasn't anyone she had met. Not someone from her college, not a neighbor, not a storybook prince. But he existed in the corner of her world like a shadow that walked just behind the light.

She had never spoken about him. Not even to herself in the mirror.

He didn't speak either—not in sentences or conversations—but she understood him. Understood the pauses, the stillness, the tug in her chest when she stood alone on the balcony and felt like she wasn't.

Sometimes, when she sketched late at night, the charcoal lines would guide her hand without her knowing why. A figure would appear — tall, unfinished, always facing away. He would be standing beneath a sky smeared in indigo, or beneath trees that bent with the wind as though they knew he was there

One evening, she stood in the garden alone.

The porch lights were flickering. The jasmine creepers had bloomed unusually early. The scent was almost dizzying.

She closed her eyes and whispered under her breath, *"Do you think they'll notice this time?"*

A pause. Stillness.

Then a breeze lifted the hem of her kurta, and she smiled faintly, like someone had answered.

Inside the house, laughter echoed. Someone was calling her name.

She turned and walked back, the smile disappearing just before she crossed the doorway.

To her parents, Radhika was doing well. She worked diligently, kept her room tidy, and called her grandmother every Friday.

To Anay, she was as quiet as always. Maybe a little more distracted. A little more intense. But still Radhika.

No one noticed that she never referred to herself as "I" anymore in her journal entries.

She had started writing in the second person.

"You walked into the rain today without your umbrella again. He likes the way water blurs everything..."

One afternoon, she stood at the construction site, watching the skeletal structure of their township project rise against the grey sky. Everyone was wearing safety helmets. Everyone was moving, working, pointing.

She stood still.

Then turned to an empty corner of the plot and smiled softly.

Anay, reviewing a checklist a few meters away, saw her.

Just a smile.

It looked beautiful. Not odd. Not strange. Just peaceful.

He didn't think much of it.

That night, she drew again.

She sketched a boy walking into a river. Only his back is visible. The sky behind him was full of birds flying in strange, impossible shapes. On the edge of the river, a girl stood with folded hands.

She captioned it in a small, careful script:
"He does not walk with me. But, it still feels like he's holding my hand."

Sometimes, she heard music in silence. Not loud. Not chaotic. Just faint flute notes, like wind passing through an old reed. She hummed along absentmindedly.

Once, her friend asked, "Is that from the film we saw?"

Radhika blinked. "No... it's older."

She didn't explain.

The day she met Anay on the terrace again, it had been raining.

He handed her an umbrella.

She shook her head. "He prefers the rain."

"Who?"

She paused for a breath too long and nodded her head and slightly blushing. Then smiled. "No one."

He laughed, confused but charmed. "You're weird, you know that right?"

"I know," she said. Then walked ahead, rain clinging to her like poetry.

Later that night, as Anay sat with Shirish again, nursing cups of filter coffee and planning the next week's site visits, Shirish asked, "You've grown quieter these days."

Anay shrugged. "Just thinking a lot."

"About her?"

He didn't answer.

He didn't need to.

Shirish leaned back and said something that would stay with Anay for years.

"Some people are born with music in their veins, but no one to dance with. Don't try to become the music. Just be the silence they can rest in."

Anay didn't fully understand it then.

But he would.

Someday.

V
THREADS OF AN UNSPOKEN YES

The garden had forgotten the echoes of old conversations, but the silence stayed—loyal and undisturbed.

Evenings came early now, slipping in like secrets. The bougainvillea vines draped lower over the gate, as though bowing in reverence to time. The same garden. The same chairs. And two people are still learning how to sit beside each other without changing the shape of the moment.

She sat in her usual spot, sketchbook open, her fingers moving without instruction. There was something in her today—not a mood, not a thought, but a hum. An invisible rhythm only she could hear. Her eyes drifted often, not towards anything in particular, but somewhere further—an inward sky, a silence she had grown fond of.

Anay watched her from the patio door. The same chipped blue mug rested in her hands. The same curl of hair was tucked behind her ear. Yet something was shifting. Not in a way one could point to, but in the way shadows stretched when no one's watching.

She had been drawing more lately. Trees without roots. Boys without faces. Moons resting in places no sky had room for. Her notebooks were quiet rebellions. No one noticed. Not really. And she didn't say much either. Her parents thought she was just more introspective. His family thought she was just shy. Only the wind that fluttered the pages of her sketchbook seemed to know better.

She began to dress differently. Lighter colours, softer fabrics. She hummed more. Sometimes a bhajan, sometimes something that sounded like it had been sung centuries ago.

Seema noticed. "You seem... happier," she said one evening.

She smiled and said nothing.

She had never known love like this. Love that didn't demand to be seen. Love that bloomed quietly, rebelliously, like wildflowers in cracks.

She had fallen. Deeply. Absolutely. With the kind of conviction only those who've loved an idea can possess.

She didn't question his absence. Because to her, he was never absent.

He was always just there.

And as the evening grew longer, and the stars blinked slowly into being, she sat on the porch—eyes closed, smile gentle—and whispered something only he could hear.

And from across the garden, Anay looked at her.

He didn't hear the whisper.

But he felt the distance.

Something had changed.

The silence between them still existed.

But now, it belonged to someone else.

Later that week, the monsoon arrived—soft and unannounced. The garden welcomed it like an old friend. Petals unfurled. The swings glistened with drops. And somewhere between the stillness and the stir, something began shifting in Anay's world too.

He had always been steady. Predictable. The boy with organized shelves, a tidy inbox, a curated music playlist. But lately, he had been slipping—forgetting meetings, staring too long at pages that didn't turn, mistaking rain for thunder even when the skies were gentle.

It wasn't a heartbreak. Not yet. But the anticipation of it.

He could sense it in the way she walked lighter now. In how she looked content with nothing in particular. In how she didn't flinch at the thought of being alone. There was a fullness in her solitude now. One he didn't belong to.

He wanted to ask her. Wanted to understand.

But the same silence that once comforted them now stood between them, guarding whatever she had begun to hold dear.

In the corner of her sketchbook, a figure appeared again. More formed this time. Defined features, eyes that mirrored oceans, a slight smile that felt like home. She colored in his presence like she was remembering, not imagining.

Shirish, too, began noticing things.

He once found her standing in the hallway, whispering. When asked who she was talking to, she laughed it off. "Just a story I'm building," she said. He didn't press further.

Seema overheard her speaking in her sleep. Soft murmurs. A name. A promise. Something about the stars.

Anay heard none of this. But he saw her smile from across the room at no one. And once, when he called her name, it took her a full five seconds to return to the moment.

He told himself she was just distracted. Caught up in her creative world. He told himself many things.

But every time she excused herself to the porch with her sketchbook, he felt it again—that ache of not being enough.

She never wrote his name. Never drew him. Never once did she speak of love to him.

Yet he loved her.

With the quiet loyalty of the moon—always present, even when unseen.

One evening, Anay found her humming in the kitchen while making tea. The tune was unfamiliar, ancient almost. Their fingers brushed briefly when she handed him his cup. She looked at him then—really looked—and for the first time in weeks, he thought he saw something flicker.

A softness.

A pause too long.

That night, he replayed it again and again.

Was she beginning to see him?

Could it be?

Even their parents noticed the change. One afternoon, Seema nudged Rajan with a smile as she walked in carrying plates. "She's grown fond of him, hasn't she?" Seema said.

"It seems like it," Rajan replied, glancing at them. "They look... easy together."

Anay's parents weren't blind either. They saw how she lingered longer in conversations when he was around. How her silences around him were softer. More filled. They mistook her distant smiles for shyness. For blooming love.

Later that day, he left a note in her sketchbook. Not a confession. Just a line—*"If I were a colour, I'd choose to be the one that makes your skies clearer."*

He didn't sign it.

But he hoped she'd know.

The following evening, she looked at him with a certain light in her eyes. Anay felt his chest expand with a quiet hope.

But then she turned away—and whispered something to the wind.

And smiled.

Not at him.

At someone else.

And Anay, standing in the golden spill of dusk, felt it again—the ache.

She wasn't falling for him.

She was in love.

But with whom—he didn't know.

On a particularly humid evening, while their families sat around retelling old vacation stories, she stepped out onto the garden path barefoot. Her dupatta trailed behind her like a ribbon of air. The rain had just stopped, and the earth steamed beneath her toes.

Anay followed her with his eyes.

She tilted her head up to the sky and smiled.

He stood, took a step forward—then stopped.

Because she was already speaking.

To someone he couldn't see.

And as the wind rose gently, lifting the corners of her sketchbook lying on the bench, Anay understood something he couldn't yet explain.

This wasn't a phase. Or a passing fancy.

This was love.

But not for him.

And though she hadn't chosen it, and neither had he—something sacred had shifted.

He stepped back into the house, letting the door click softly behind him.

In the garden, her laughter bloomed.

And so did the wildflowers.

Her laughter had always been rare. But today, it bloomed like a reluctant flower finally touched by spring. It spilled out of her like a secret escaping—fragile, bright, and startling. The garden around her felt lighter, like it too was exhaling after holding its breath for too long. Anay noticed it. Everyone did.

She sat beneath the gulmohar tree, its blossoms mirroring the vermilion warmth of dusk. Her dupatta fluttered behind her like an unfinished sentence. The sun filtered through the leaves above, casting trembling shadows on her face—half-light, half-longing. She laughed again, this time at something Kabir said, and her eyes crinkled at the corners, not from joy, but from the force of holding something deeper inside.

From the verandah, Seema and Rajan watched her. Rajan, arms folded and thoughtful, whispered to his wife, "She's smiling more around him now. Do you see it?"

Seema nodded, but her eyes were tired. "Yes. She's... changing."

And inside the Joshi household, a shift was silently forming—one that had nothing to do with love and everything to do with misunderstanding it.

Anay stood at a distance, watching her. His heartbeat had grown to echo her smallest joys. A glance. A smile. Even a shared silence. Everything felt like a beginning to him. A prelude to something written only for them.

Earlier that week, she had asked him if he liked rain. That's all.

But to him, it was everything.

He had walked home that day with damp shoes and a heart soaked in foolish hope.

Even Amruta noticed. She playfully ruffled Anay's hair one morning and said, "You've been floating these days.

What's going on in that engineer's brain?"

"Nothing," he said, grinning.

But his father, Shirish, raised an eyebrow. "Nothing? Then why did I hear you humming in the shower yesterday? You haven't done that since you were thirteen and obsessed with that cricketer."

Anay chuckled, shook his head, and ducked away.

Later that evening, the two families sat together for dinner. It has become a weekly ritual now. Rajan and Shirish were discussing the final leg of their business collaboration, and Amruta had brought out her signature mango shrikhand.

"You're spoiling us again, Amruta," Seema smiled.

Seema laughed, but then her eyes flickered to Radhika, who was sitting quietly beside Anay, picking at her food with a far-off look in her eyes.

She had been like this for weeks—drifting, smiling at things unsaid, giggling at jokes no one had told.

And once, just once, Anay caught her looking at him in a way that made his breath stutter. Like she *saw* him. Not as a friend. Not as a family's son. But as *something more*.

He held onto what looked like a secret.

But something else had begun to bloom in the undercurrent.

A strange softness in Radhika's gaze—never consistent, always unexpected. She would look out of the window and smile. She would pause while stirring tea, as if someone had whispered something only she could hear. Once, she even murmured a line under her breath, a line Anay couldn't catch, and when he asked her, she blinked and said, "Did I say something?"

No one noticed the way her reality had started to shift ever so slightly—just enough to blur the edges between what was and what wasn't.

To Seema and Rajan, it looked like maturity, emotional growth.

To the world, it looked like a girl finding peace in the arms of familiarity.

That night, as Anay lay in bed, he scrolled through old photos on his phone. There she was—smiling in group pictures, half-hiding behind a pillar, sitting on a bench with a book in her lap. Every image carried the weight of his quiet longing.

He remembered their last conversation that evening. She had asked him if he believed people could fall in love without even realizing it.

He smiled. "Yeah. I think sometimes the heart notices before the mind catches up."

She didn't respond.

Just stared at him with a strange kind of softness in her eyes. He fell asleep thinking she was falling for him.

Radhika had started to look at him differently. Or so it seemed.

She lingered longer in conversations with him. Smile softer. Sometimes she seemed to forget there were others in the room when he spoke. And her gaze—searching, always, like she was watching someone behind his eyes.

It wasn't love, the way Anay had dreamed it. But it looked like something.

Everyone began to talk.

Not overtly. Not publicly.

But in glances exchanged between parents. In pauses between dinner and dessert. In suggestions dropped like seeds.

She found herself listening to the conversations that floated through the air at night like half-forgotten lullabies. She would smile when his name came up. Laugh, sometimes, without realizing. And when she walked past the neem tree he often sat under, her steps would falter ever so slightly—as though waiting.

But the truth was quieter.

Because inside Radhika, something had changed. Something had bloomed without sunlight, in shadows and solitude.

There were moments—tiny, almost imperceptible—when she would look at Anay and not blink for a little longer than necessary. When her fingers would twitch slightly as if tempted to reach out, then retreat. When her breath would hitch at his proximity, but not because of him. Because of something else. Someone else. Someone who didn't exist outside of her.

And then came the day Seema sat beside her daughter and held her hand.

"Radhika," she said, voice trembling under the weight of something that had been waiting too long, "we think... It might be time to think about the future. You know Anay. You've known him. He's kind. He understands you."

Radhika looked down.

She didn't speak. But she didn't shake her head either.

"You don't have to say yes right now," Rajan added gently. "But we think it's something beautiful. Something safe. And it's what people are already seeing."

What people are already seeing.

That was it.

She hadn't said she loved Anay. Not once. But she hadn't denied the feeling that was being reflected back to her either.

Because how could she?

How do you explain that the thing you feel isn't for someone who exists?

How do you deny love when the world is already calling it pure?

How do you confess that sometimes, when Anay stood in front of her, she saw someone else—not in his place, but as though overlaid, like a transparent memory she couldn't erase?

And so, Radhika didn't say no.

She said nothing at all.

And the silence, like most silences in her life, was misinterpreted.

So the preparations began. Quietly. Cautiously. Like touching a wound you don't know exists yet.

The news moved like a ripple through their circle. The Joshi-Lele wedding. Two families, already close, now bound by something deeper. Something beautiful.

Anay was told in the same garden, under the same tree. Amruta had cupped his face, her voice warm and proud. "She said yes, Anay. Radhika. She's going to be your wife."

He didn't speak. Not at first.

He didn't run, either.

He just sat there for a long time after his mother left, staring at the neem leaves falling like tiny eyes from above.

Because somewhere in the stillness of Radhika's eyes, he thought he saw it too.

He didn't know that she was looking at someone else inside him.

Someone she thought only she could see.

He didn't know that her heartbeat echoed for a name never spoken aloud.

And so the world mistook madness for affection, silence for consent, and a hallucination for love.

The days turned warm with ceremonies.

Henna on her hands. Music humming through the courtyard. Anklets singing on the stone floors. Jasmine in her hair. Bangles clinking like soft applause. Families blending laughter and rituals into something sacred.

Radhika wore the weight of the upcoming wedding like a silk dupatta—too light to protest, too embroidered to ignore.

She smiled when spoken to. She nodded when asked. And every time Anay looked at her, his heart dared to believe.

It was the dream he had carried for years. The love he had planted like a secret and watered with silence.

And now it was here.

Or so he thought.

Because she did look at him. Her eyes held something new. Something soft.

Even Seema had whispered to Rajan one evening, as they watched Radhika thread marigolds, "Look at her. She's... different these days. Happier. It must be Anay."

Radhika would wake in the middle of the night sometimes, with her hand placed gently over her chest, as if calming something that fluttered there. She couldn't explain it. The sudden rush of warmth, the vivid glimpses in her dreams of someone speaking to her without words.

It wasn't Anay. But she couldn't tell them that.

Because they believed.

And so, beneath the laughter, under the music, between blessings and bangles, a story continued to fold itself quietly—

The kind that doesn't unravel until it's too late.

VI
BETWEEN ANKLETS AND ECHOES

The moment the families agreed on the engagement, a quiet celebration sparked through both households like ghee catching flame—gentle, sacred, and full of promise.

Amruta's voice was the first to lift in joy, calling out to the women of the family to start preparing for the rituals. Seema, ever the poised planner, moved swiftly from one room to another, her bangles chiming like temple bells. Even Shirish and Rajan, usually grounded in practicality, allowed themselves the rare indulgence of excitement. The date was chosen. Auspicious, they said. The ninth day of the waxing moon. A good day to begin.

Marigolds began to appear everywhere—looped around door frames, strung above windows, tucked between mirrors. The air turned fragrant with haldi and sandalwood. Women gathered for mehendi discussions and song rehearsals. Every space hummed with a golden kind of anticipation.

Radhika watched it all unfold from a distance.

The engagement was set under the soft canopy of a winter afternoon.

Sunlight filtered through strings of marigold and mango leaves, casting golden patterns on the courtyard tiles. Women in silk sarees moved like petals in a breeze—green, orange, purple—each drape catching the sun, each anklet chiming like laughter made visible. The scent of sandalwood and gajra mingled in the air, sacred and familiar.

Radhika sat on a low wooden platform, her saree the color of twilight—indigo with silver embroidery so delicate it shimmered when she moved. Her hair was braided in the traditional Marathi style, jasmine tucked neatly along the curve. The nath on her nose—pearl-tipped and crescent-shaped—glinted as she looked down, her hands folded softly in her lap.

There was something ancient about her.

Like she had walked out of an old Peshwa painting. Regal, yet distant. Present, but unreadable.

Beside her, Anay wore a cream-colored kurta with a matching Nehru jacket. His hair was neatly combed, forehead marked with a small chandan tilak. He looked at her not as a man claiming love, but as someone reverently receiving a miracle he hadn't dared ask for.

The priest's voice rose above the hum of the courtyard, chanting mantras in rhythmic waves. Rice grains. Kumkum. Sugar crystals. Rings carried in silver trays. Elders whispered instructions. Children peeked through railings. Cameras clicked gently like raindrops on windows.

It was the evening before the engagement day

Her laughter had bloomed again.

But this time, it wasn't the soft echo under the neem tree or the polite giggle shared over chai. It was brighter—startling in its warmth, yet edged with something that lingered too long. Like a flower opening out of season, radiant but aching against the chill.

She stood in the courtyard that evening, the sky melting into a thousand shades of copper and violet. Children ran past her, anklets jingling, their mirth unburdened. Somewhere behind her, the elders discussed wedding silks and mandap decorations. But Radhika was still.

It was Amruta who noticed her first—her head tilted slightly to the side, eyes not on the horizon but slightly above it, as if listening to something just out of reach.

"She's glowing," Amruta whispered to Seema. "It's like she's in love."

Seema smiled, fingers tightening over the wedding card samples in her lap. "Maybe she finally understands what she's getting. Maybe it's Anay."

Everyone seemed to believe it.

Even Anay.

Especially Anay.

He had caught her staring at him during lunch. She hadn't looked away. Her gaze had softened—not playful, not curious, but distant, like a dream halfway remembered. And Anay, whose heart had lived so long in restraint, dared to believe.

He began to think it was happening. That maybe, finally, she was beginning to feel the same. That the silence between them had ripened into something tender.

He didn't know that she was watching someone else—someone layered over him like the memory of a shadow, someone whose name she never spoke, even to herself.

She had started to write again.

Small verses on scraps of paper. Folded napkins. The margins of old books. Lines that made little sense to anyone else. Metaphors that bent logic but whispered of longing. Her journal filled with stardust and rivers, of eyes that never blinked and voices that weren't voices at all.

She walked slower now, especially through places where light filtered in—like something unseen was guiding her feet. She whispered to herself sometimes. Not always with words. Often with silences.

Once, Seema found her standing alone in the middle of the living room. Just standing. Hands at her sides. Eyes open. Not blinking. As if she had forgotten what she was doing, or worse, remembered something no one else could see.

But when asked, Radhika only smiled. A smile that curled around truths too heavy to say aloud.

And then, the preparations deepened.

The guest lists were finalized. Gold threads were chosen for her blouse. The date was inked in red on the calendar. Every moment moved forward with the weight of certainty.

Radhika didn't stop it.

Not because she agreed.

But because there was no one to whom she could confess that her love was not meant for someone who lived in this world.

And because the one she saw didn't really exist.

But everyone thought it was Anay.

Even Anay thought it was him.

And she—she had no words left to separate illusion from intention.

Her heart ached in ways that felt ancient. Like she had loved someone in another life and their echo was returning through Anay's presence. Her parents mistook it for emotional depth. Her friends called it poetic. The priest said it was destiny.

And Radhika—she only kept moving forward, caught in the quiet tide of expectation.

She didn't argue.

She didn't rebel.

Because how do you argue with ghosts?

How do you reject a marriage when the world thinks you're already in love?

And how do you confess you're seeing someone no one else can?

She stood one evening by the window, watching the sun disappear like a secret. Her reflection merged with the sky behind it. And for a moment, she whispered a name.

Not Anay's.

But nothing came out.

Only a sigh, soft and cracked, like a page tearing in an old book.

Downstairs, Shirish was laughing with Rajan about the rituals. Amruta was folding sarees into careful stacks. Anay stood by the staircase, adjusting his cufflinks, rehearsing a smile.

And Radhika—

She closed her eyes.

Next day, it was the time when Radhika lifted her hand for the ring, it trembled only slightly.

Anay didn't notice.

But Seema did. She reached forward and steadied her daughter's wrist for a second too long, brushing her thumb across Radhika's pulse as though reading a truth even she couldn't admit.

Then the ring slipped on.

The applause came. Laughter, whistles, claps.

Amruta's eyes filled with tears. Shirish clapped Anay on the back. Rajan called for sweets. Friends teased the couple gently. Photos were taken—portraits of a joy that everyone believed in.

Radhika smiled for each one.

Sometimes she forgot that the camera couldn't catch what her eyes were really looking at.

Sometimes she forgot she was supposed to be happy.

But there was comfort in the rituals. Like the world was offering her a rhythm to follow. A choreography to hide in.

The women sang lavnis in soft voices as trays of modaks and puran polis were passed around. The sounds of dholki tapped in the background. Elders sat cross-legged on white mattresses, dipping spoons into basundi, retelling stories of their own engagements in the 80s.

Anay leaned toward her only once.

"You look like a dream," he whispered.

She looked at him. She really looked at him.

And smiled.

Not because she believed it.

But because he did.

And sometimes, that was enough to keep the illusion breathing.

Later that evening, Radhika sat alone in her room, her ring hand resting on a diary she hadn't opened in weeks. The silver shimmer of the ring danced in the moonlight. A symbol of love she didn't feel, but couldn't refuse.

She whispered a thank you to the silence.

To the version of love that had kept her heart alive, even if it had no form in this world.

Outside, fireworks cracked like distant promises. Families clinked glasses of paan sherbet. Anay's voice mingled with her father's.

And Radhika closed her eyes again.

Letting the ring glow gently on her finger—

Like a borrowed star meant for a different night sky.

The courtyard had begun to glow in the faint orange hush of dusk. Fairy lights weren't yet strung, but the household felt like it had already lit up from within. There was a hum in the air—of preparation, of joy, of names being paired in casual conversations like they'd always belonged together.

Radhika had been quieter these days, but not in the way Anay had known her silence. This was different. Not empty, not uncomfortable. Just... somewhere else. Like her gaze was stitched to a place slightly beyond the moment. Slightly beyond him.

It had been during the saree selection.

Seema had laid out the pastel silks like watercolour dreams on the bed—peach, sea green, butter yellow. Anay had wandered into the hallway, purely by accident, when he heard her laugh—an actual, full laugh—and paused.

He peeked in gently. She was seated, one leg folded beneath her, holding a lavender saree to her chest, smiling at someone.

But the way she tilted her face... the softness in her eyes... the way her fingers lingered on the pallu like she was imagining someone brushing it back from her shoulder—it hit him. Like déjà vu. Like someone had replaced his name in her daydream with someone else's.

"Who were you talking to?" he asked later, as they stood side by side, sipping warm chaas under the soft gold of evening.

Radhika blinked, startled. "No one."

And then that smile. The kind that closes doors instead of opening them.

Anay didn't ask again.

But his heart had folded that moment and hidden it somewhere unreachable.

Because to accept the truth would mean accepting that perhaps this wasn't the love he had waited for. Perhaps the warmth she gave him wasn't meant for him.

But then again—maybe it was nothing.

Maybe it was just bridal nerves, or the daze of upcoming changes. Maybe she was tired.

Maybe love sometimes wears unfamiliar masks before it shows its real face.

So he held on tighter. To the idea. To the illusion. To the long-cultivated belief that she was his, and had always been.

And yet.

There were little things.

The way she smiled at empty balconies. The way she whispered into the wind. The way, during the haldi prep, she had absentmindedly touched the swing in the verandah, like someone had just been sitting there.

Anay had looked too. But the swing was still.

The world was beginning to make space for a presence that didn't exist.

Or worse—only existed in Radhika's world.

VII
THE WEDDING AND THE WIND

The engagement had left the Lele and Joshi households wrapped in the fragrance of marigolds, cardamom tea, and shared dreams. The families, once tied only through business, were now embracing a bond far deeper. There were more visits, more chai served in porcelain cups, and more laughter that sounded like home.

Radhika started coming over to Anay's house more often. She helped Amruta pick out curtain shades for the new living room. She made notes for Shirish's anniversary surprise for his wife. She carried herself like an ideal to-be bride—measured, soft-spoken, kind, always doing just enough to win hearts, but never enough to reveal her own.

Amruta doted on her with quiet joy, and Shirish teased Anay when she wasn't looking. "That girl will run this house better than you ever could," he'd say with a chuckle, elbowing his son.

Anay would smile. But his eyes stayed on Radhika, trying to trace the space between her presence and her absence. She was there, yes—but like a song you hum but don't know the words to.

One late afternoon, the sun was melting into orange behind the old gulmohar tree, casting warm splinters of light into the Joshi home.

Radhika sat on the porch steps beside Rajan, the two of them wrapped in a blanket of quiet that only years of understanding could knit. A cup of lukewarm tea sat untouched beside her.

Rajan looked at her profile—how the wind tucked strands of her hair behind her ear as if even nature wanted her to look less distracted, less lost.

"You're very quiet today," he said.

"I'm always quiet," she replied, barely turning her head.

"But today your silence is louder than usual," he said softly, with a father's instinct that had learned to read the spaces between her spoken words.

She turned toward him, her eyes tired but gentle.

"Do you remember," she began, "when I was little and you used to call me your little moon?"

"Of course," Rajan smiled. "Because you never liked to be out during the day. You'd wait until the sun was down to talk, to laugh. My little moon bloomed in silence."

She chuckled, and the sound was brittle, like an old song playing from a cracked radio.

"I'm still like that, Papa," she whispered. "Only now, I don't know if I'm moonlight or shadow."

Rajan didn't answer at first. He reached over, gently placing his hand over hers. "Shadow only means there's light somewhere. And I know you, Radhika. You don't speak unless you're speaking to something deeper."

She leaned her head on his shoulder, the same way she used to as a child after reading a sad story.

"I'm supposed to be happy," she said.

"You don't have to be 'supposed' to feel anything," he replied. "But tell me, beta... are you happy?"

She closed her eyes.

"I think I am."

That small, simple sentence ached in the space between them. It wasn't a lie. But it wasn't the whole truth either.

Rajan sighed, brushing her hair behind her ear.

"You know, your mother and I—when we first got married—we didn't know what love meant. But over the years, love found us in the quiet mornings, in shared cups of chai, in silence that didn't need to be filled. Maybe it's not about what love looks like when it begins. Maybe it's about what it grows into."

She nodded, a tear slipping down, unnoticed by either of them.

"But Papa..." she said after a while, "what if... the thing I feel... doesn't grow into anything the world can accept?"

He looked at her then. Not with worry. Not with fear. But with the softness of a man who had raised a girl with stars in her head and storms in her chest.

"Then you love it anyway," he said. "Even if the world never does."

A silence followed. The kind that didn't feel empty, but full.

"I want to make you proud," she whispered.

"You already do."

She smiled then—fragile, trembling, but real. And he kissed her forehead, holding her like he used to when she was afraid of monsters under her bed.

Later, the night was soft with silence, the kind that sits on your shoulder and breathes in rhythm with your heartbeat. The marigolds hung tired but fragrant. The lights blinked drowsily as if trying not to disturb the sacred hush that had fallen over the world.

Alone in her room, Radhika sat cross-legged on the cool marble floor. The bridal saree draped carefully over the nearby chair whispered promises of a future she wasn't sure belonged to her. The soft hum of distant laughter drifted in from the veranda, wrapping her room in a haunting contrast—joy outside, silence within.

And then— a knock. Gentle. Rhythmic. Like the sound of a heartbeat on glass.

She turned.

There he was.

Madhav.

No grand entrance. No announcement. He appeared the way some truths do—soft, certain, and impossible to ignore. The monsoon breeze stirred as he stepped closer, and it wasn't just wind—it was memory, breath, a presence far too real for something unreal.

He looked just as she remembered. Or imagined. Or needed. Hair slightly tousled, shirt creased like he'd walked through every story she'd ever told herself. His eyes carried the calm of someone who'd seen the world and still chose silence. And his smile—oh, his smile—it was carved from the same sky that bore dusk.

"You called," he said gently, the corners of his lips lifting in quiet affection.

"I didn't mean to," she replied, her voice smaller than usual, like it might shatter the moment.

"But you did."

They sat on the floor, knees just touching—barely—enough to feel each other's warmth without breaking the sacred air between them. No need for candles or rituals; the space between them glowed in ways chandeliers never could.

Madhav reached for her hand but paused inches before contact. A hesitation not out of fear, but reverence—as if to say: *This closeness is already enough.*

"Will you marry him?" he asked, his tone not accusing, not sad. Just curious. Honest.

"I have to," she replied after a pause that seemed to stretch lifetimes.

"Do you want to?"

She looked down at her lap. Her bangles chimed, soft and tragic, like wind chimes in a storm.

"You know already know my answer"

Madhav's smile didn't falter, but the light in his eyes dimmed—not from heartbreak, but from understanding. That rare, painful kind. The kind that lives quietly in all things inevitable.

"We weren't made for temples or vows," he said. "We were the pause between verses, the glance before the confession, the ache that came with beauty too big for words."

She nodded slowly. "And you won't stop me?"

He shook his head. "Would you stop the tide from kissing the shore? Would you ask twilight not to fall?"

He leaned closer, the scent of rain and sandalwood clinging to his presence. "Let them bind you in rituals. I'll remain in the unspoken—between your breath and your becoming."

"I'll wear the saree, I'll smile in photos," she said. "I'll become what they need me to be. But I'll keep you—here." She touched the spot over her heart.

"And I'll live there," he whispered. "Where no name is needed. Where no label fits."

Madhav rose slowly, the kind of rise that felt like dusk unfolding over a quiet lake. He reached down and smoothed a crease in her saree—not with touch, but with gaze, the kind of gaze that rewrites every memory without changing a word.

"You'll be a good wife," he said. "But don't let them tame the wild in you."

She smiled, soft and secret. "Only if you promise to stay."

"I'll be the rain on your windowpane. The last note of your favorite song. I'll be the silence between your thoughts."

And then,

he vanished as if he wasn't there in the moment

No door creaked. No curtain lifted.

Only the scent of jasmine lingered, and a curtain that swayed like it had seen something divine.

The room didn't mourn his absence. It held it.

Radhika sat for a long while, her hands in her lap, her shadow long against the floor.

It didn't hurt anymore.

It hummed.

Not with closure.

But with a love too eternal to need an ending.

The engagement had lit the fuse of celebration, and now, the house pulsed with the joy of preparation. There was turmeric in the air, marigold strings hugging every corner, and the fragrance of fried besan and melting jaggery wrapped around every visiting soul like a warm embrace.

From the moment the date was decided, it was as if the entire Joshi and Lele households had begun to dance. Sangeet rehearsals echoed through hallways. Aunties fought lovingly over song choices. Little cousins performed dramatic renditions of film love stories.

Haldi was a golden riot—laughter flowing as easily as the turmeric paste on the couple's cheeks. Radhika sat glowing, her face radiant not from makeup but from memory, her eyes soft as if watching someone no one else could see. But she smiled when Anay smiled. She blushed when he teased her. She laughed when the haldi got in her hair. To the world, she was the image of a woman in love.

Batata wada crackled on open flames. Glasses of panha clinked cheerfully. Sweets—so many sweets—lined the tables: puran poli rich with ghee, modaks with coconut and jaggery folded like tiny dreams, halwa glistening with love and roasted dry fruits.

The sangeet was an evening dipped in amber light and joy. Radhika wore green, like the first whisper of spring. Anay watched her dance, watched the way her anklets sang louder when she moved. She laughed into the night, and he believed, with everything in him, that he had found happiness.

Because from where he stood, it looked like love.

But there were moments. Just flashes.

When her gaze wandered—away from him. When she tilted her head like listening to someone no one had addressed. When she smiled as if she was answering a question no one had asked.

He ignored them.

Until he couldn't.

The night before the wedding, he caught her by the veranda, standing in her bridal lehenga for the final fitting, looking at the sky as though it were whispering something sacred.

"Radhika," he said gently. She turned, startled, and then smiled, wide and open.

But in that split second, he saw it. Not disinterested. No doubt. But... distance.

She looked through him, not at him. And for the first time, a name surfaced in his heart that he hadn't dared speak aloud before.

Madhav.

He didn't know where it had come from. He didn't know what it meant.

But it pressed itself into his thoughts like a thumbprint on glass. Familiar. Incomplete.

Anay said nothing. He didn't question her. Didn't accuse her. Because love, his kind of love, wasn't a courtroom. It was a temple—quiet, patient, waiting.

And so the day dawned bright, almost too perfect.

The wedding was a burst of marathi celebration. The mandap bloomed with jasmine and mango leaves. She wore a Paithani that shimmered like rain-washed gold. He arrived on a white horse, reluctant but regal, drowned in rituals and rose petals.

There were conch shells and ululation. There were a hundred hands blessing them, a thousand eyes watching them.

Radhika looked beautiful.

Radhika looked complete.

And yet—

Somewhere in the hidden corners of her mind, Madhav stood, hands folded behind him, smiling. She saw him. Not beside her. But within her.

Anay tied the mangalsutra around her neck. She didn't flinch.

Sindoor found its way into her parting. She didn't blink.

The cameras flashed. The crowd cheered.

And just like that, they were married.

Everyone was happy.

Amruta wept quietly. Shirish patted Anay's shoulder like he was proud of the man he had become. Seema and Rajan embraced their daughter, convinced she had found the love she deserved.

But even in the heart of all that joy, as fire circled and vows were spoken, Anay's eyes found her again.

And this time, when she smiled at him—he smiled back.

But only half.

The air outside the mandap was heavy with rosewater and sandalwood. Lanterns swung from the trees like warm suns caught mid-dream.

Inside, the ceremony had begun.

Anay sat beside her, his sherwani stiff with zari embroidery, palms tinged yellow from haldi that still carried the scent of turmeric and camphor. Around them, chants bloomed into the evening like soft thunderclouds rolling through a golden sky.

Radhika looked divine.

There was no other word. Her saree—navvari draped with the precision of an ancient rhythm—clung to her like a forgotten melody. Her jewelry sparkled not with the cold pride of gold, but with the quiet blessing of legacy. Her smile was gentle, folded at the edges like a secret prayer.

And yet—

There was something in her gaze that night. A softness too far away to be touched. A stillness that didn't belong to the world around her.

She wasn't beside him.

Not truly.

Anay watched her as she adjusted the edge of her saree, as she bowed her head before the sacred flame, as she folded her hands during every mantra. She did everything right. She looked the part. Played it to perfection.

But every now and then, her eyes flicked toward something... or someone.

Someone who wasn't there.

And it hit him.

Madhav.

The name he had only heard in whispers inside his own mind.

Never spoken.

Never proven.

He had no reason. No logic. No evidence.

Just a quiet thread of intuition winding through his chest like smoke curling through a broken window.

Anay didn't flinch. Didn't speak. Just turned his face back toward the flames and listened to the sound of ghee crackling in the sacred fire.

He told himself he was imagining it. Those weddings were overwhelming. That love—even when returned—could sometimes feel lonely.

But he also knew—

Radhika's silences weren't empty.

They were filled with someone else.

Still, he said nothing.

Because what was there to say?

What kind of man questions love on the day of its arrival?

But in her heart, something else bloomed.

Something no ritual could bless. No priest could bind.

It wasn't defiance.

It wasn't betrayal.

It was something older than them both—*a love with no beginning and no name*, that didn't ask for permanence, only presence.

And Madhav—wherever he was—must have smiled then. Not with jealousy. But with that quiet knowing only imagined lovers carry.

The conch blew. The drums roared. A thousand marigolds fell like sun-colored rain.

Anay looked at her one last time before stepping off the mandap.

She smiled back.

And for a moment, everything looked perfect.

Perfect enough to last.

But somewhere behind her smile, behind the bridal glow, behind the haldi and the vermilion...

Later, all were dancing and enjoying, a little dramatic like the films and between the scenes even she was dancing,

dancing with someone else.

And Anay knew.

He knew.

But he chose not to stop the music.

Not tonight.

Because sometimes love is not about possession.

Sometimes it's just about staying, even when you're the only one dancing to the song.

VIII
UNFOLDING

They had been married for three days.

The sindoor in Radhika's hair was still fresh, like a wound yet to scab. Her bangles chimed with the sound of new beginnings, yet each note held an echo of a song Anay didn't fully recognize.

Their bags were packed with silks and expectations, perfumes and protocols. The morning of their departure gleamed with sunlight and ceremonial farewells. It was their first trip as husband and wife—what the world would call a honeymoon. The air was filled with a celebratory sheen, like the warm gold stitched into Radhika's shawl as she stepped out of the Joshi home, her anklets singing quietly.

The original plan had been Himachal Pradesh—snow-laden hills, luxurious spas, and pine-scented chalets booked months in advance. The idea of mountains and seclusion, of champagne breakfasts and scenic views, had pleased Anay's family, and Anay too, to an extent. But somewhere in between wedding rituals and whispered prayers, Radhika's voice—so soft it could've been mistaken for breath—had added two more destinations to their itinerary.

"Vrindavan… Mathura," she said, almost dreamily, not as a suggestion but as a confession.

No one questioned it. How could they? She looked so serene when she said it, as though the very syllables of those places offered her a kind of invisible anchor.

Anay had nodded, accommodating, the way a man in love nods even when he doesn't fully understand. But inside him, something flickered. No doubt. Not quite. But the smallest sliver of unease—as if his heart had just missed a beat it usually never does.

They flew —Shirish Joshi wouldn't allow his son and daughter-in-law to travel any other way. The flight hummed over cities and clouds, and still, between them, sat a strange, unacknowledged silence. It wasn't uncomfortable. Not tension. Just something… thick, like honey, like unanswered prayers.

Anay watched her from across the aisle.

Radhika sat by the window, chin in hand, looking out at the sky like she was searching for something in it. She had been quieter since the wedding. Not sad—no, she smiled often, asked polite questions, and responded with grace. But it was as though her spirit was always elsewhere, dancing somewhere a few steps ahead of her body.

Their first destination—Vrindavan—appeared beneath them like an old poem. From the air, the land looked like a patchwork quilt of temples, trees, and time. The minute they stepped out of their car, a sweet dust clung to their skin. The scent of sandalwood and marigold was thick in the wind, bells echoed from corners you couldn't see, and every wall seemed to have once listened to prayers.

Vrindavan, the land of legends and unspoken tales, greeted them with its soft, eternal grace. The streets, narrow and winding, were a labyrinth of time—every turn seemed to lead to another memory, another whisper of the past. The air held the delicate scent of sandalwood and marigold, carried by the breeze that rustled through the banyan trees, their ancient roots clinging to the earth like the stories of the souls who had walked here before.

The soft dust of Vrindavan, kissed by the endless sun, seemed to have a golden glow that clung to the skin like a blessing. Every temple, every pillar, every stone in this sacred town seemed to breathe with the weight of devotion. The temples themselves were works of art, their stone carvings intricate and delicate, their walls adorned with centuries-old frescoes depicting scenes from the Bhagavad Gita and the Radha-Krishna legends—timeless, radiant, yet imbued with an almost mystical sadness.

The Yamuna River, winding like a silver thread through the land, shimmered under the fading light of the day. Its waters, rippling with whispers of the divine, seemed to carry the very essence of the place—a serene, almost otherworldly calm that settled in the heart like a quiet prayer. Along its banks, ghats glowed with the soft light of hundreds of diyas, their flames flickering and dancing with the rhythm of the evening breeze.

As the sun dipped below the horizon, the evening air turned cooler, and the golden light that bathed the land became richer, more honeyed. The sound of temple bells rang through the air, clear and resonant, echoing against the ancient walls. The smell of incense drifted from the small shrines nestled in every nook and cranny, filling the air with a sacred sweetness.

The streets came alive in the soft, fading glow of twilight. Pilgrims in saffron robes walked slowly, reverently, their faces serene as they made their way to the temples. Cows, sacred and calm, wandered lazily through the lanes, their slow movements in sync with the pace of the land itself. Children played with marigold petals, and the distant sound of a flute—so delicate, so haunting—carried on the wind, as if the very essence of Krishna was alive in every note.

The town had a quiet, almost palpable energy—alive with devotion, yet filled with a sense of calm, of stillness, as though time here moved in gentle waves rather than a relentless forward march. It was a place where the divine seemed to merge with the mundane, where the sacred and the everyday lived side by side in perfect harmony. Here, under the infinite sky and amidst the timeless beauty of Vrindavan, Radhika seemed to be connected to something older, something far beyond the present moment.

Radhika lit up, in a way Anay hadn't seen her do at their wedding.

She walked through the alleys like she remembered them from another life. Barefoot on temple floors, her dupatta flowing like a memory, she closed her eyes when the conch blew at Banke Bihari Temple, as if the sound touched a part of her no one else could access.

They stayed in a luxury haveli, one restored with regal arches and sprawling courtyards, adorned with antique teak furniture and jasmine garlands. Every morning began with the soft murmur of bhajans, and every evening closed with the call of peacocks in distant orchards.

And yet, Anay couldn't find rest.

He tried. He did.

He reached for her hand during walks, complimented her quietly, arranged for candlelit dinners in private balconies, where the Yamuna glistened below. But she seemed somewhere else. She smiled—but it was the smile of someone whose heart was already in conversation with another world.

One evening, as they strolled along the ghats, she paused by a murti of Krishna. The light of diyas reflected in her eyes. She bent down to offer flowers, and when she stood up, there was a glow in her that startled Anay.

Not joy.

Reverence. Familiarity. Longing.

As if she had just returned home.

Anay's hand remained at his side.

He didn't ask what she prayed for.

Back in their haveli, she sat by the jharokha window, hair open, eyes distant. She wasn't unhappy. She wasn't anything that could be named.

He watched her from the threshold of the room, something stirring in his chest again. Not yet a suspicion. Not yet fear. But a deep, echoing quiet.

She turned to him with a soft smile.

"It's peaceful here, isn't it?"

"It is," he said.

But inside, his gut whispered—Peace should not feel this far away.

And so, while Vrindavan bloomed around them in jasmine and chants, and the town folded itself into twilight, Anay stood at the edge of something unnamed, wondering if love could look like prayer, and if devotion could sometimes be meant for someone else entirely.

The days in Vrindavan stretched like silk, each moment slipping quietly, unnoticed, through their fingers. Anay tried to hold on, to anchor himself in the serenity of the place. Yet, something—something intangible— hung in the air, brushing against his senses like a soft whisper. It wasn't the city itself. It was Radhika.

The journey from Vrindavan to Mathura was shorter than it should have been. A quiet, unspoken transition, as though the sacred dust of Vrindavan had left something behind—a weight in the air that neither of them acknowledged, but both could feel. The sun rose over the fields as they drove, painting everything in hues of gold and amber, but Anay barely noticed the beauty around him. His mind was tangled with thoughts he hadn't yet given voice to.

The silence that had settled between them during the flight seemed to have expanded in the car, an almost palpable thing that clung to them, thick and unquestioned. Radhika stared out of the window again, her face turned towards the passing landscape as if it was a place she'd once known deeply. She wasn't speaking to him much—nothing unusual, he thought—but today, the stillness felt different.

Radhika's silence was not new. It had always been a part of her, a quiet depth he could never fully reach. But now, it felt... far. As if she were listening to a distant, echoing voice no one else could hear.

The early morning light wrapped Mathura in an ethereal glow. The town felt older than Vrindavan, steeped in centuries of stories yet untold. The lanes, even narrower than before, were lined with little temples and shrines, hidden in every corner. The air, thicker with the scent of incense and oils, seemed charged with something invisible. Anay felt it immediately—a kind of presence, something out of place but undeniably strong.

It wasn't just the temples. It was Radhika.

As they walked through the narrow streets, Radhika seemed to glide, her feet barely touching the ground. The air around her shimmered, and Anay felt an odd twinge in his chest, a kind of unease he couldn't explain. She moved from temple to temple, her fingers brushing over ancient stone carvings, her eyes closing as though she were communicating with something unseen. She stopped at each one, pausing just a beat too long. It wasn't reverence that held her there; it was something else.

At the Shri Krishna Janmabhoomi temple, where a crowd had gathered to offer prayers, Anay noticed her standing at the entrance, her hand resting lightly on the cool stone of the temple walls, her body still, her gaze distant. She appeared lost in a thought that wasn't her own, and for a moment, Anay caught the soft curve of her lips—like she was listening, but not to the people around her.

When he reached for her hand, his fingers brushing against hers, she didn't immediately respond. It was as though she hadn't even noticed him. A flash of panic rose in his chest, but he pushed it down quickly, offering her a smile that she didn't quite return. Instead, she turned away from him, her footsteps leading her deeper into the temple complex, her hand trailing along the walls as if searching for something only she could find.

He followed, trying to keep pace, but she moved faster. Her movements were almost fluid, the way someone might walk when they are in a trance, caught between worlds. Anay's stomach churned. It wasn't just the quiet that disturbed him anymore. It was the growing sense that she wasn't with him. That she hadn't truly been with him for a long time.

Outside the temple, by the narrow steps leading to a smaller, hidden shrine, Anay saw her again—standing in front of a marble statue, her expression soft and tender, like she was in the presence of someone she deeply cared for. Her lips parted slightly, as if she were speaking, though no sound came. The sun had started to set, and the sky was painted in shades of pink and lavender. The golden light of the evening reflected off the marble and the surrounding architecture, creating a dreamlike atmosphere.

Anay approached slowly, his heart racing, unsure of what he was seeing. As he drew closer, Radhika turned her head slightly, her eyes meeting his for the briefest moment. There was something in that glance, a fleeting recognition of him, but it was quickly replaced by something else—something far deeper, far more knowing.

She spoke softly, almost to herself, "He's waiting."

Anay froze. The words struck him like a cold gust of wind. His mind raced, but before he could ask her to elaborate, she turned away again, her fingers brushing the statue, her gaze returning to the marble figure with an intensity that left him breathless.

His feet moved on their own accord, stepping closer, yet still hesitant. He had no idea what was happening. The man he had married this woman to seemed to be slipping further from him with each passing moment. A strange kind of dread began to coil in his chest, tighter and tighter, and his mind urged him to find answers, but the answers felt like they were just out of reach.

Radhika had always been a bit ethereal, a woman of mystery, of depth, but this? This was something else entirely. She had always been lost in thought before, but this felt like she was lost in another world altogether.

Anay tried to hold onto the logic that had always guided him, but it slipped from his grasp, like water through his fingers.

"Radhika..." he began, his voice sounding more like a question than a statement, but she didn't respond. She simply continued her silent conversation with the statue, her eyes fluttering closed again, her lips moving in quiet, inaudible whispers.

The world around them seemed to fade into the background as Anay stood there, watching her, helpless. His suspicions were growing. He couldn't deny it anymore. Something was changing. Something was different about Radhika, and he didn't understand it.

Later, when they reached a small ghat by the river, he saw her standing by the water, a soft breeze lifting her hair. Her expression had softened to something intimate—an understanding only she shared. She stood motionless, almost entranced, and as she lowered her gaze to the waters, Anay saw something in her eyes that he couldn't place. It was a look that felt both foreign and familiar at the same time—like a secret shared between her and someone else.

Anay's heart pounded in his chest. The unease had now turned into something more—something raw. He could feel the weight of her detachment pressing down on him, and every moment he spent in her presence seemed to push him further away from her. This was no longer just a quiet moment in their marriage. It was something darker, something unsettling.

He approached her, but this time, she didn't turn to him. Instead, she spoke softly, her voice barely above a whisper. "It's all around me here, Anay... Can't you feel it?"

He didn't answer. He couldn't. The words lodged in his throat, replaced only by a hollow, gnawing sensation that grew stronger with each passing second.

As they continued through Mathura, the presence of whatever was in her mind—whatever or whoever she was seeing—became undeniable. Anay could feel it in his bones now. And with it, came the quiet, insistent urge to uncover what was happening to his wife.

The hills of Himachal waited, but Mathura refused to let go.

The air in Mathura had grown denser, like breath behind a closed door. Radhika moved through the sacred city with the grace of someone slipping back into something once lost. She floated through temple corridors and quiet alleys like she belonged to them. Like they had been waiting.

She smiled more now. But not at Anay.

She disappeared more too. Not with deception, but with ease, as if vanishing into thin air was a ritual she had rehearsed a thousand times.

"Just a short walk," she would murmur.
"Only a few flowers," she'd add.

But the silences between her words felt colder than the stone steps of the ghats.

Anay watched.
And then he followed.

It wasn't jealousy that made him do it.
It wasn't fear.
It was the ache of the unknown—loud and unruly, like rain before a thunderstorm.

He wrapped himself in a shawl, his face half-covered, as he slipped through the streets of Mathura. Every corner echoed with chanting, the scent of camphor, and temple bells singing like haunted memories. The walls whispered stories older than memory, stories that clung to him like incense smoke.

He walked with eyes wide open—heart thudding louder than any prayer.

And then—he saw her.

Draped in soft ivory, she moved ahead, oblivious to the world, to him. Her dupatta whispered along the dusty path as if it had secrets of its own. She turned down a narrow lane—a part of town untouched by tourist feet.

Anay followed, step by step, pulled by something he didn't yet have words for.

The lane narrowed further, walls closing in like secrets. It opened finally into a small forgotten courtyard, where time seemed to exhale and rest.

She stopped before an ancient temple, overgrown with silence and wild bougainvillea. It wasn't on any map, not the ones they'd planned, anyway. The kind of temple that's forgotten by time but remembered by souls.

She walked in. Alone.

Anay stayed behind a peepal tree, breath sharp, his knuckles white from gripping the iron gate.

He peered inside.

She was standing before the altar—but not quite facing it. Her eyes weren't on the deity. They were angled slightly to the side, fixed on nothing. And yet... filled with emotion. Her lips moved, slow and soft, shaping words meant for someone who wasn't there.

He stepped closer. Leaves crushed beneath his feet. Still, she didn't flinch. Didn't turn. Her world was sealed.

And then he heard her.

She laughed—quiet, familiar.
She tilted her head, listening.
She replied to someone.

His rage coiled.
Who was she talking to?
Who had she come to meet?

The storm inside him surged. The betrayal he never imagined began to bloom like poison ivy around his ribs.

He pushed the gate gently—it creaked.
He stepped in, not hiding anymore. The fury in his veins needed a name. A face.

She didn't notice him. Her hands moved like they were tracing the air. She whispered something again.

Anay took a few steps closer.

And then—he stopped.

His breath caught.
His heartbeat slammed.
His world fractured.

There was no one there.

No one beside her. No shadow. No silhouette.
Just Radhika.
Talking.
To emptiness.

But her face—her face was lit up like she was in the arms of someone who knew her deepest name. Her voice trembled with affection, with devotion, with... recognition.

Anay's fists unclenched. His body didn't.

What was this?
What *was* he seeing?

The anger curdled into confusion.
Then fear.
Not fear of betrayal.
Not anymore.

But of something far more terrifying.

She wasn't lying.
She wasn't hiding.

She was... believing.

He stepped back. A twig cracked beneath his foot.

This time, she turned.

Their eyes met.

Anay—mouth parted, questions clawing at his throat—wanted to scream, ask, demand.

But Radhika only smiled.

That same distant, serene smile—the kind one wears when they've seen a miracle no one else can.

He opened his mouth. But nothing came out.

He was too late. Not just to follow. But to understand.

And in that silence, something irreversible passed between them.

Anay turned and walked away, not out of choice—but because staying felt heavier than the storm inside him.

What he saw wasn't a secret lover.
It was something stranger.
Something sacred.
Something unspeakable.

And yet, as he walked away from that temple, he felt the truth follow him like a shadow—silent, faithful, and growing.

IX

A Thread
Unraveled

They left Mathura, but Mathura hadn't left Anay.

Their journey to Himachal wasn't rushed—not the kind that needed airports and boarding passes. It was deliberate, almost symbolic. Anay had insisted on driving himself. A long road trip. Just the two of them. No drivers, no interruptions. He told Radhika it would be romantic—windows down, old Hindi songs, tea from highway dhabas. She nodded with a smile that barely reached her eyes.

The car was a luxury SUV—sleek, black, fully loaded with a sunroof that filtered the mountain light and leather seats that seemed too elegant for the weight of silence they were about to carry.

They took the NH-44 route, stretching through Agra, Delhi, and Chandigarh before weaving into the folds of Himachal. Hours passed as the terrain shifted from dusty plains to the first green blush of foothills. Outside, pine trees swayed in harmony, clouds descended like silk veils, and monasteries clung to hilltops like secrets. Inside, there was a quiet unlike the usual tired silences between travelers. This silence had weight. Shape. Direction.

Radhika slept beside him, head resting gently against the window, her features softened by the filtered light of a sun trying to peek through mist. She looked peaceful. Almost too peaceful. As if her dreams were made not of this world, but another.

Anay drove, the steering wheel gripped tighter than needed.

His mind was a storm.

The temple. Her whispers. The way her eyes shone for someone who wasn't there.

The smile.

He hadn't asked her about it. Couldn't. Not because he lacked the courage—but because he lacked the language. What do you even ask someone who speaks to shadows with the intimacy of old lovers?

They passed small villages painted with mustard fields, tea stalls with flickering bulbs, and old temples perched at the edge of cliffs. At one point, they paused at a roadside dhaba for cutting chai and pakoras. Radhika barely touched hers. She stood at the edge of the gravel lot, eyes on the distant hills as if waiting for something—or someone.

He watched her, the unease growing like fog inside his chest.

Back in the car, she drifted into sleep again.

And then he noticed something. A diary. Half-tucked in her bag.

He didn't reach for it. Not yet.

But he began to google.

Talking to someone who isn't there.
Smiling at invisible companions.
Conversations with imagined people.
Delusions or... schizophrenia?

The results opened slowly, page by page, each headline clawing at his insides.

"Schizophrenia: Signs and Symptoms."
"Hallucinations and Emotional Detachment."
"Paranoid and Grandiose Delusions."
"Can someone love a person who doesn't exist?"

His breath hitched.

He looked at her again. This time, not as his wife, not as the girl he loved since childhood, but as a puzzle whose pieces didn't fit where they once had.

And yet...

He couldn't hate her.

Even now, there was something sacred about the way she slept. As though the universe itself had wrapped her in gentle protection.

They reached Himachal by dusk. The mountains stood tall like ancient gods, and snow dusted the roads like forgotten memories. Their luxury resort overlooked a deep valley, the wooden chalet gleaming with amber lighting, fireplaces roaring, the scent of pine needles infused with the quiet hush of snowfall.

She awoke just as they arrived.

Her first words were, "It's beautiful."

But her eyes weren't on the mountains. They were in the sky. Wide and empty.

Anay smiled back. But it was a smile stitched with worry.

Inside, the suite was draped in elegance—plush throws, silk curtains, copper bathtubs, and every comfort money could buy. But no warmth could fill the cold that had crept between them.

That night, she stood by the window, hair untied, staring at nothing. Humming softly. A tune he didn't recognize.

He watched her from the reflection in the mirror.

Radhika had never looked more radiant.

And yet, never more distant.

He pulled out his phone again, refreshed the tabs.

Schizophrenia. Visual hallucinations. Emotional isolation. Fixation on imaginary figures.

His chest sank with every word. Each one a raindrop in the flood he hadn't prepared for.

But still, no answers. No confirmation.

Only questions. Unformed. Untamed.

She turned to him suddenly, mid-hum.

"Did you say something?"

He shook his head.

She smiled, then turned back to the window.

And all he could think was:

If there's someone else in her world... where do I even begin to find him?

The present hummed between them like an old, frayed wire threatening to snap.

Kabir stared at Anay across the dimly lit rooftop, his tea untouched, lips parted in disbelief.

"So the schizophrenia symptoms you asked me about... you said it was for one of your employees," Kabir said, his voice sharp with quiet hurt. "But it wasn't for any employee, was it?"

Anay looked away for a moment, as though the night sky could offer him the words he hadn't yet found. His jaw tensed.

"It was for Radhika."

Kabir exhaled slowly, as if the truth itself knocked the wind out of him. "Damn it, Anay. Why didn't you tell me earlier? Why didn't you come to me again? You think I wouldn't have helped you?"

"I didn't know what I was looking at," Anay said, voice low but thick. "I didn't even know how to form the question."

Kabir's frustration brimmed like a glass too full. "You should have said something. You were watching her unravel alone?"

"I wasn't watching her unravel," Anay said quietly, "I was trying to hold her pieces together before I even knew she was breaking."

Kabir's breath hitched, his anger softening just slightly at the weight behind those words.

Anay leaned forward, eyes dark, jaw set. "I called you to ask about symptoms because my gut wouldn't let me sleep. I had to know what I was seeing. I needed names for the ghosts I was chasing."

Kabir sat back, silent, letting it sink in.

Anay continued, his voice steadier now, like a man finally ready to walk through fire.

"She didn't stop in Mathura. Even in Himachal... he was there."

Kabir blinked. "Madhav?"

Anay nodded.

"His presence never diminished. If anything, it... thickened."

They had arrived in Himachal to the hush of pine trees and the perfume of snow. Anay had chosen the kind of mountain retreat that echoed luxury—heated floors, glass windows that opened to the Himalayas, a private chalet kissed by snowfall and silence.

But peace never came.

Radhika moved through the rooms like she was visiting a museum of someone else's life. Her footsteps were soft, aimless. Sometimes she'd disappear for hours—walking in the woods alone, or lost in the town nearby.

She began scribbling in a leather-bound journal she carried everywhere. At first, they were just sketches. Birds, temples, anklets, flute-like spirals. But later—words. Names. Conversations she never had with him.

At night, Anay would hear her murmuring in her sleep. Sometimes laughing softly, sometimes calling out. One night, he leaned in close, his breath caught in his chest.

She whispered, "Madhav... don't leave me. Not now."

The name hit him like thunder under his skin.

He began noticing patterns—how she lingered too long at temple bells, how she touched certain tree trunks as if they held secrets, how her fingers danced midair while she stared at empty corners.

He once caught her, sitting on the wooden bench near the orchard behind their suite, smiling at the wind, lips moving in hushed conversation.

He stood inside the glass door, just out of sight, watching her speak with no one. Her head tilted like she was listening. Nodding. Laughing. Then silence.

She placed something on the bench beside her—a wildflower crown she had woven with her fingers.

As if placing it on someone's head.

Anay didn't know whether to step outside or stay frozen.

He chose silence.

That night, he picked up her journal after she'd fallen asleep.

The latest page had no drawings.

Only a line repeated over and over.

"He is the only one who hears me."

Anay sat beside her sleeping frame, heart pounding like a drum carved from grief.

He didn't confront her.

Not yet.

But at that moment, the word schizophrenia stopped being a theory.

It began to feel like the truth.

And yet, who was Madhav?

Was he a figment?

A fantasy?

A metaphor?

Or something else?

The room filled with the warmth of firewood, but Anay shivered.

Because in all his searching, all his questions...

He still didn't know—

If she was sick... or simply in love with someone he couldn't see.

Anay could feel the shift in the air. It wasn't just the biting cold that lingered over the Himachal hills; it was something else, something gnawing at him from within. Radhika had become a mystery he couldn't unravel. And the further they moved from Mathura to the quiet isolation of the mountains, the harder it became to ignore the growing unease in his chest.

She wasn't the woman he had married. At least not entirely. There were pieces of her slipping away in ways he couldn't grasp, and he wasn't sure if he was afraid of losing her—or afraid of what would be left when she was gone.

In the mornings, they would wake up in the cottage tucked between the snow-dusted pines, the soft sounds of nature filling the spaces between their words. Yet, despite the idyllic beauty around them, there was a silence between them now. A quiet that stretched for miles, where the only thing Anay could hear was the pounding of his own heart.

Radhika was present—physically, at least—but emotionally, she had already stepped into another world. The world she visited when she disappeared into the woods, when she stared out the window for hours, lost in thoughts Anay couldn't follow. It was as if she was slipping through his fingers, and no matter how much he reached, she was always a few steps ahead.

Anay had become acutely aware of her odd behaviors. Sometimes, she would scribble in her notebook, her face intent on some invisible thought. Other times, she would hum songs he couldn't recognize, songs that seemed to speak to something in her, but he couldn't quite reach. It was almost as though the fabric of reality around her had started to warp.

She would laugh softly to herself in the kitchen, and when he asked what was so funny, she'd smile and shrug, as if the moment had passed. *"Nothing,"* she would say,

"Just something I remembered."

And though Anay didn't want to admit it, the more he watched her, the more he realized there were moments when her eyes would drift, unfocused, as if she were looking at something—or someone—no one else could see.

One day, as they walked along the snow-covered path leading to a nearby temple, Radhika stopped. Anay was just behind her, not far enough to be unnoticed, but still, she hadn't spoken since they'd left the cottage. It was unusual for her to be this quiet.

"Are you okay?" he asked, his voice low but laced with concern.

She didn't answer immediately. Instead, she turned her face up toward the sky, the snowflakes gently falling onto her dark hair. For a moment, she was still, as if listening to something just beyond his reach.

Then, softly, she spoke. "I remember a place like this... a long time ago. The snow. The silence. The way it feels to be close to someone."

Her words weren't directed at him, and yet, they struck him like a chord being plucked, sending a chill through his spine. Was she remembering something? Someone?

"Radhika..." he began again, his heart pounding. He wanted to ask her more, but her eyes were distant, her gaze fixed on something invisible. Something only she could see.

She nodded slowly, as if in answer to a question he hadn't asked, and then continued walking, never once looking back at him.

Later that evening, he found her by the window again, staring into the dark expanse of the mountains. The fire crackled in the hearth, casting long shadows across the room, but she didn't seem to notice. She was too far gone in her own thoughts.

"Are you planning on telling me what's going on with you?" Anay's voice broke the silence, but even as the words left his lips, he knew they sounded desperate. Almost accusatory. He regretted them immediately.

Radhika didn't respond right away. She just continued to sit there, her fingers lightly tracing the edge of her notebook. Finally, she spoke, her voice so quiet he almost didn't hear it.

"I'm fine, Anay. Really. It's just... sometimes the world feels so far away. Like I'm standing on the edge of it, looking in."

Her words were cryptic, and they sent a strange shiver down his spine.

Days passed, and the unease in Anay's chest only grew. He tried to push it down, tried to convince himself it was just the stress of the wedding, the change of pace, the isolation. But deep down, he knew there was something more. Something far deeper than what he could put into words.

She had started talking in her sleep. Not loud enough for him to catch everything, but there were times when she would murmur names, snippets of conversations, her voice full of warmth. Sometimes, she'd smile, and for a fleeting moment, it was as if she was *with* someone—someone who wasn't him.

Her smile wasn't the same as before. There was a softness to it now, an unspoken familiarity that he couldn't place. It wasn't him she was smiling at. It wasn't him who she whispered to in the dark. It wasn't him she was holding close.

Anay's chest tightened. He had caught her in those moments more than once. And yet, when she woke, she would seem so unaware. She would smile at him and go about her day, as if everything was normal, as if he hadn't seen the *glance* that wasn't meant for him.

It was that night, as he lay in bed, staring at the ceiling, that he understood. Or at least, he thought he did. He didn't have the clarity he needed, but the pieces were starting to fit together.

He remembered a conversation he had with Kabir weeks ago, the way Kabir had warned him of the danger of *ignoring the signs*. The signs he had refused to acknowledge.

Now, everything—the whispers, the distance, the disappearing acts—made sense.

Schizophrenia. He didn't need the confirmation from Kabir anymore. His heart sank as he realized it. This was what was happening to Radhika. And despite all the love he had for her, despite all his care, he didn't know how to save her. Or if it was even possible to save her.

Her world, her reality, was slipping away, and he had no idea how to bring her back.

She had gone beyond his reach. Beyond any logical place he could stand. Her mind was a labyrinth, and she was lost within it, and he was standing at the entrance, unable to find the key.

He turned his back to her side of the bed, trying to push the thoughts from his mind. He was tired. So tired of fighting the darkness that hovered just at the edges of their love. But as he drifted off to sleep, the final question lingered—haunting him.

What was he supposed to do now?

X
PILGRIMAGE OF THE HEART

Back in Mumbai, the city had resumed its relentless rhythm. Cars honked with familiar impatience, buses sighed against their brakes, and somewhere in the background, a distant train cut through the city's clutter like a memory refusing to fade. The air buzzed again with humanity—vendors calling out, children shouting after one another, the television sets glowing behind curtainless windows.

But high above it all, in Anay's bunglow, silence sat like a deity—unmoving, all-knowing, and absolute. Adding to it, his parents had gone for a vacation now, to offer the couple privacy and some more time to spend.

It wasn't the silence of emptiness. No. It was full—of held breath, of quiet reckonings, of moments gathering like clouds before a monsoon. It wrapped itself around the furniture, settled over his shoulders, and nestled in the corners like an old friend.

Anay sat still.

Not on his usual plush couch in the main lounge, but on the smaller, older two-seater by the floor-to-ceiling window—where the view of the Arabian Sea stretched like a painted illusion. The waves moved in rhythm, unaware of human turmoil, uncaring of stories unfolding behind the glass.

His phone lay face down on the coffee table in front of him. A playlist he had meant to play blinked from the screen—paused. It was supposed to be music to soothe him, to anchor him back into routine. Instead, he had chosen something else.

He chose to listen.

To the unremarkable, uncelebrated rhythm of time.

The ticking of the antique wall clock—gifted to them by an uncle who said it had survived wars.

Tick.

Tock.

Tick.

Each second was a heartbeat. A drumbeat. A whisper.

And Anay... he smiled.

But it wasn't the smile of contentment. It wasn't peace. It was the slow, dawning smile of a man who, after days of drowning in questions, feels the first brush of air on his face. A smile cracked open by exhaustion. By revelation.

He wasn't doing anything. No call. No journal. No pacing. Just sitting.

But it was the most alive he'd felt in days.

The sea moved. The clouds passed. The clock ticked. And he remained—a still point in a churning world.

It was in that stillness that the answer came to him—not crashing, not dramatic, not shouted from the heavens. But like the first light that seeps under a locked door. Quiet. Steady. Inevitable.

He would understand.

Not fixed.

Not cure.

Not saved.

Just... understand.

That was the beginning.

He had spent so many days trying to hold onto the version of Radhika he knew.

The girl who twirled her dupatta when nervous.
The woman who always double-knotted her shoelaces.

The bride who, on their wedding night, asked if she could leave the windows open to hear the sound of the city even while asleep.

But somewhere along the journey—from love to marriage to mystery—Radhika had quietly stepped into a different world. Not out of betrayal. Not out of malice. But perhaps out of necessity. And he, in all his love, had tried to pull her back into his.

He'd held on to her fingertips like she was drifting away on some invisible tide. Tried to anchor her with conversations, gestures, even silence. But nothing worked.

Because he was trying to speak in one language, while she was living in another.

And now—sitting in a city that felt loud and muted all at once—he realized that all this time, he had been looking for her in the wrong dimension.

Radhika wasn't gone.

She was *elsewhere*.

And if he truly wanted to find her, to meet her elsewhere—he had to stop being the husband who felt left behind.

He had to become the friend who walked beside her—even if the path made no sense to him.

Even if it led into the forest of madness.

A friend she could confide in, not just when the world was watching—but especially when it wasn't. A friend who wouldn't try to fix her, or understand her through diagnosis, but someone who'd sit beside her and say, *"I don't understand, but I'm here."*

And to do that...

He needed to know.

Not the superficial definitions he had skimmed during the trip. Not the articles he half-read between confusion and fear. But the depth. The soul of it. The living, breathing complexity of what she was going through.

He stood slowly, crossing the quiet marble floor of the apartment, the sun pouring in golden through the sheer curtains.

The laptop sat on the dining table, closed, like a book waiting to be read.

He pulled the chair, sat down, and opened it.

The screen came to life.

His fingers hovered over the keyboard—not with hesitation, but reverence. As if what he was about to type was no longer mere research.

It was a pilgrimage.

He typed:
"Conceptual delusions in schizophrenia."
The search bar blinked.

Then:
"Imaginary companions in adults."
"Schizophrenia and emotional projection."
"Anthropomorphizing a feeling into a person."

The results flooded in—case studies, medical journals, research papers, forums.

He dived in, headfirst, heart in hand.

He read about how some patients form *emotional relationships* with non-existent people, how these companions often offer comfort, understanding, and love—the very emotions reality has failed to provide.
How these figments aren't "hallucinations" in the way people think—but extensions. Embodiments of feelings that never found a home.

Madhav.

Her silence began to take shape now. Her distant smiles. The softness in her voice when no one was around. The scribbled names in her notebook. The flicker in her eyes at temples, as if someone had just entered the room and she was the only one who saw him.

He listened to a podcast of a woman who described how her companion, a man she had named after a book character, had been with her since childhood.

"He's not just in my head," she had said. "He's in my heart."

Another paper spoke of *delusional emotional anchors*—how love, when it cannot exist outwardly, creates an inward substitute.

Radhika wasn't just imagining someone.

She was *in love* with someone she had created.

And what's more—he was beginning to see *why*.

Madhav was probably everything Radhika needed—kind, comforting, understanding, always present, and most importantly—*hers*.

Where reality could be cruel and unpredictable, Madhav was safe. He was the embodiment of all the love she had once wished for but never received in full.

Anay's eyes welled up as he kept reading. Not out of pity. Not from grief.

But awe.

It was heart-breaking, yes.

But it was also... sacred.

What he found over the next two hours didn't just change how he saw her. It changed how he saw the world. The fragility of the human mind. Its beauty. Its defense mechanisms. The stories we tell ourselves to survive.

And the stories we fall in love with.

He closed the laptop slowly. The light outside was fading into a soft apricot. The sky held that moment before dusk—when it looked unsure whether to surrender to night or hold on to day just a little longer.

He looked at the empty seat across from him.

And whispered into the hush,

"I'm coming for you, Radhika. Not as your husband. But as your best friend."

And suddenly, the silence in the house didn't feel so heavy.

It felt like a beginning.

A sacred pause before the symphony.

A plan was forming—not one of fixing, but of understanding. Of listening.

He didn't know how long it would take.

But he knew now *why* he must do it.

He stood up, heart steadier, spine straighter, and walked toward the room where she slept—alone, and yet not.

And he, finally, felt like he was about to meet her.

It wasn't just about understanding anymore.

Now it was about becoming.
Becoming someone, she could see when the world around her slipped away.
Becoming the truth behind her illusion.
Becoming the warmth behind her whispers.
The *real* behind her *imagined*.

If her mind had given birth to a Madhav—if this presence, this echo of devotion, had wrapped itself so gently into her soul—then Anay knew he couldn't erase it.

But maybe...
Just maybe...
He could *replace* it.

Not by force. Not by logic. But by *feeling*.

He would not stand at the shore and pull her back from the storm.
He would walk into the waters with her.
Let the madness soak his bones.
Let the fog swallow him too—until she didn't have to walk it alone.

The plan didn't start with steps or bullet points.
It started with listening.

Not to words, but to silences.
The way she paused at corners as if someone else would turn with her.
The way she smiled at the wind like it whispered secrets.
The way she looked out of windows as if waiting for someone only *she* could see.

Anay began to join her in those silences.

He sat beside her during her long stares and never interrupted.

He stood behind her gently when she was scribbling on notepads, not reading, just watching—watching the strokes of someone trying to birth a parallel universe on paper.

Sometimes she would hum a tune he had never heard, but always in the same tone—like a lullaby from another world.
Anay memorized it.
Hummed it in the shower.
Played it softly on the piano, not asking where it came from, just honouring that it existed.

That *he* existed.

He began to *become* Madhav, piece by piece, not in delusion, but in devotion.

He stopped calling her by name in rushed moments—he whispered it instead, like the wind did.

He left notes on her mirror, not as husbandly reminders, but poetic questions:

"Did the stars keep you warm last night?"
"If the sky could speak, what would it tell you today?"

He started showing up in places she didn't expect.

Not following her, but *finding* her.

At bookstores she wandered aimlessly.
At parks where she sat alone on swings meant for children.
At cafés she never told him about but always visited on Thursdays.

He would sit across the room, not speaking.

Sometimes she would look up and see him.

And for a moment, just a blink, she would stare at him like she *knew him from somewhere else.*

A small, puzzled smile would dance across her lips, and then fade before she said anything.

That was enough.

At night, he stopped holding her like a husband does.

He just lay next to her.

Breathing slowly.
Letting his presence speak louder than touch.

Sometimes she spoke in her sleep.

Not always words—just sounds.

But once... once she said:
"I knew you'd come, Madhav."

And Anay didn't flinch.

He didn't cry.

He didn't shake her awake.

He just whispered back:

"I never left."

And still, he read.

He studied.

He built a secret library inside himself.
A library of her—her movements, her patterns, her poetry, her drawings, her music.

He created a journal—one no one else knew about—where he sketched the shape of her madness not to escape it, but to live inside it.

One page read:

"If her mind is a house with broken windows, I will sit beside her and build paper curtains. If there are monsters in her attic, I will bring them tea. If she talks to shadows, I will learn their names."

Another read:

"If Madhav is her safe place, I'll knock gently and ask if I may come in too."

It wasn't about proving anything to her.

It was about earning the truth.

He knew she wasn't ready to tell him about Madhav.

And that was okay.

Because when you truly love someone, you don't wait at the gate demanding entry.

You plant wildflowers outside the door, so when they do open it—there's beauty waiting.

And so, Anay began.

Quietly. Deeply. Softly.

Not just planning to help her.

But preparing to *become* a part of her beautiful delusion—

Until one day, gently, she might realize:

He was never outside of it at all.

He looked out the window that night.

The sea, dark and infinite, mirrored his heart—full of waves, unsure of shores.

But something stirred in him now.

A kind of light.

A *hope.*

He was not lost.

He had a direction.

Not to bring her back to the world...

...but to meet her in hers.

To meet her not as Anay.

But maybe—

Someday—

As **Madhav.**

XI

The Unseen Serenade

Anay decided it was time to explore the origins of Madhav—not in a clinical, detached manner, but in a tender, curious way. Like someone tracing the outline of a beloved's childhood sketch, he wanted to understand what made Radhika's heart choose him, build him, and love him.

But he knew the story wouldn't be found in any journal, nor revealed through questions. It would come like birdsong before sunrise—unexpected, fragile, and only if he remained still enough.

So he softened his presence around her—like rain that doesn't announce itself but still soaks the soil. He didn't bring up Madhav directly. There were no confrontations, no weighty conversations. Instead, he offered companionship in small, quiet ways.

He'd help set her brushes in the right place before she began painting. He'd leave a hot mug of her favorite coffee beside her sketchpad without a word. He started laughing more when she did, even if he didn't understand the joke. He wasn't decoding her anymore—he was simply being with her.

Some evenings, they'd sit by the balcony, city lights like scattered stars beneath their feet. Radhika, lost in the hush between words, would sip her tea slowly. And Anay, with a warm patience, would offer questions disguised as wonder.

"Do you think someone can love you even if they've never met you?"

She smiled faintly, not looking at him. "Maybe that's the purest kind."

"Did you ever have an imaginary friend when you were little?" he asked another time, as they watched raindrops trace lines on the glass.

She looked at him sideways, a glimmer in her eyes. "Not just one. But one that stayed."

Sometimes she'd answer with a smile. Sometimes with silence. But slowly, the silences began to soften. To trust.

One night, under a sky full of monsoon clouds, she spoke.

"It wasn't a moment," she said, her voice almost caught in memory. "It was more like... a breeze. You don't see where it starts. You just feel it, and suddenly everything is moving."

Anay didn't flinch. He just listened. Every blink was a prayer for her to keep going.

"There were days I didn't want to be in the real world. Days when everything felt too loud, too confusing. And then, one day... I imagined someone sitting with me on that old bench under the banyan tree near my school."

She paused.

"I didn't give him a name at first. But he listened. He looked at me like I mattered. I think that's when he began."

Anay's heart twisted—not with sadness, but reverence. She was handing him pieces of herself, slow and sacred.

He didn't ask who it was. He didn't need to know yet. This wasn't about *Madhav* the name. It was about the feeling. The need.

"Sometimes," she whispered, "I think he understood the silence better than the noise. Like he spoke the same language as my thoughts."

Anay gently nudged her shoulder with his. "Maybe you taught him that."

She smiled, wide this time. "Maybe."

The days passed like chapters unfolding in a book neither of them was reading aloud. He noticed the way her stories came wrapped in metaphors. How she still walked as if beside someone. How her laughter sometimes drifted in two directions.

And slowly, she began to let him stay during those quiet hours. When she painted. When she hummed. When she stared at a blank wall, smiling softly.

Anay never interrupted. His silence became a kind of music—a space where she could exist without explanation.

Some nights, he'd sit beside her on the floor while she worked on her canvas. They wouldn't speak. He would just be there. And she would glance at him now and then, her eyes soft, as if surprised to find him still there.

Once, as he handed her a fresh cup of tea, she looked up and said, "You don't ask much. Why?"

He shrugged. "Because I want you to tell me when you're ready. Not when I'm curious."

And she nodded, as if that answer built another brick in the temple of her trust.

Somewhere in between her pauses and his patience, a new friendship bloomed. Not built on past promises or future hopes. But in presence.

She hadn't told him everything. But she had begun.

And that beginning was sacred.

Anay wasn't trying to be her answer anymore. He was becoming the place where her questions could rest.

And in that, he was winning her heart—not as a lover. But as her safest friend.

The next morning, the sun cast a soft gold over the kitchen counter where Radhika was buttering toast. Anay wandered in, scratching the back of his head, and without a word, started slicing some fruit. They moved in rhythm, quiet yet not distant.

"You know," he said casually, "I used to think silence meant something was wrong."

She chuckled, handing him a slice of toast. "And now?"

"Now I think it means something's real."

Their eyes met for a brief second. Something passed—an understanding too fluid for language.

Later, in the garden outside their apartment, they sat cross-legged on the grass. Radhika was sketching lazily on a notebook. Anay was doodling beside her, poorly.

"What's that?" she giggled, peeking at his page.

"A dog," he said.

"That's a camel."

He laughed. "Then I guess I've made a revolutionary discovery in evolution."

She smiled, then looked at him—not with confusion, but with comfort.

"You're different these days," she said.

He paused. "In a good way?"

"In a soft way."

He looked down, suddenly shy.

"Maybe I'm just learning the right language," he murmured.

She went quiet again, and then—without looking at him—she said, "Thank you for not trying to fix me."

"I'd never dare," he said gently. "I'm just... walking beside you."

And that, in all its simplicity, was the truth.

It was a quiet evening, one of those where the sky forgets to be dramatic and simply allows itself to be still. Radhika and Anay sat on the balcony, their legs tucked under soft blankets, two mugs of warm cocoa resting on the small table between them. The world was muffled by the distant hum of the city, as if respectfully allowing their silence to breathe.

Anay watched her fingers absentmindedly trace the rim of her mug. He'd been waiting—like the ocean waits for the moon—to nudge the tide of her story closer to shore. Not out of impatience, but out of quiet longing to understand.

"Do you ever feel," he began, his voice as gentle as the breeze brushing past, "that some people were never imagined... they just arrived?"

Radhika looked up, her lashes catching the last gold of twilight. "Like they've been with you all along, even before you knew how to name them?"

Anay nodded. "Exactly that."

She smiled faintly. "There's someone like that."

He didn't lean forward. He didn't interrupt. He just let the moment stretch, like the soft unfolding of a page long folded in her heart.

"I never really told anyone about him," she said, as if confessing a prayer. "Not fully. Not because I was scared, but because it always felt like he belonged to a different part of me... the part no one ever visits."

"Maybe I could visit," Anay said, his voice tender.

She looked at him, and her eyes flickered with a soft sort of approval, like a gate gently creaking open.

"It started back when I was sixteen," she began. "There was a banyan tree outside my school. Huge. Old. It had these thick roots that wrapped around the bench beneath it like protective arms. I'd sit there during lunch... sometimes alone, sometimes pretending to read."

"And one day," she continued, "I imagined someone sitting beside me. Not speaking. Not starting. Just... there. Like he knew how to hold silence with me."

Anay's chest ached with how beautiful and intimate her words were.

"I never gave him a face at first. He was just a presence. Kind. Gentle. Patient. The type of presence that doesn't rush you to speak. He never tried to distract me from my pain. He just... sat with it. With me."

She stopped, tracing her fingers along the spine of her notebook.

"As I grew older, he became clearer. Not in a fantasy sort of way... but in a soul sort of way. Like he didn't exist outside of me, but also wasn't fully me."

"Who is he?" Anay asked softly.

She looked at him. And this time, there was no pause. No hesitation.

"Madhav."

His name was spoken like a lullaby. Like something ancient. Something sacred.

"He's... different," she continued, her voice dipping into something dreamlike. "He doesn't walk the way people do. He drifts. Like a memory. Like a song you don't remember learning but always seem to know."

"What does he look like?" Anay asked, treading carefully.

Radhika's eyes sparkled. "He looks like the sky before a storm. Wild and soft all at once. His eyes... they don't blink. They see. Not in the usual way, but in the way that makes you feel read. Known."

Anay imagined him—not as a figure, but as a feeling. A rhythm. A hum in the soul.

"He doesn't always speak," she added. "Sometimes he just smiles. Sometimes he asks strange questions like, 'If sadness had a color, what shade would yours be today?'"

Anay chuckled, but not mockingly. "What shade would yours be?"

"Grey. But the kind that comes with rain," she said. "Hopeful."

They both fell into silence again. But this time, it was a silence that felt like storytelling.

"He shows up when I need grounding," she whispered. "When I'm overwhelmed. He walks beside me, and suddenly, I'm not scared. I'm not alone."

Anay reached out and lightly placed his hand over hers. "You're not alone even when he's not around."

She smiled. "I know. That's why I can tell you about him."

The stars began to shimmer above them, not loudly, not showily—but just enough. As if they, too, were listening.

Madhav had been introduced—not with thunder, but with grace. Not as an illusion, but as a companion of the soul.

And Anay... he didn't see a threat in him anymore. He saw a door.

A door into the sacred, unspoken room of Radhika's heart.

And he was finally being invited in.

Radhika took a deep breath, her fingers trembling slightly as she placed her cup of tea down on the table. It was as though the silence of the room had enveloped her, holding her in a space where words seemed both fragile and monumental. She shifted on the couch, adjusting her posture, but Anay's presence beside her was so steady, so sure, that it almost felt like a form of comfort. She knew that now, in this moment, she was not speaking for him, not speaking for anyone, but simply letting herself be. Her voice was soft, but there was a clarity in it that hadn't been there before.

"It wasn't as if he just appeared one day," she began, her fingers curling around the rim of her cup, the warmth of the tea comforting in a way that brought her back to her younger self. "It was more like he... slowly wove himself into the quiet spaces. A shadow at first. A whisper."

Anay didn't speak, didn't rush her. His silence was like a cushion, soft and welcoming, letting her spill her heart out without fear.

She looked at him for a moment, her gaze distant as though the years between then and now had blurred into something fluid. "I was... alone, Anay. Not physically, but... there was always this distance.

A barrier between me and everything around me. People would speak to me, but their words felt like they were bouncing off invisible walls."

A light, almost wistful smile tugged at her lips. "And then, one day... It was the wind. The way it shifted, as if something had moved within me. I was sitting under that old banyan tree near school, and it wasn't really a person at first. It was just... a presence. A feeling. The kind you don't always name right away, but you know it's there, like the scent of jasmine before you can see the flower."

Radhika's eyes drifted to the window, watching the trees sway in the breeze, as if the memory was still playing in the air.

"He sat beside me. Not too close, but not far either. I didn't look at him at first. He wasn't a figure, not something solid. But I knew, somehow, he was there. It wasn't like I called him. It wasn't like he *decided* to be there. He was just... there."

She paused, and Anay noticed how her fingers gently twirled the strands of her hair, something she did when she was remembering.

"And then, one day, he spoke. 'You look sad.' I remember that clearly. Just like that. As if he knew. Not because he'd seen me cry, not because I'd told him anything. Just... he *knew*."

Anay's heart tugged, but he stayed still, letting her words pour out without interruption.

"He was always different from anyone I'd ever known. He wasn't afraid of what I didn't say. He laughed when I laughed and even more when I didn't." She smiled, her eyes twinkling a little. "He'd make the silliest jokes, and somehow, I always found them funny. In the worst moments—when I felt like I was drowning in a sea of my own thoughts—he was the one who pulled me back to the surface."

She let out a small, wistful laugh, the sound light and airy. "And he didn't care that I was... well, *me*. All the things I thought made me different, broken, or odd—he didn't even notice them. It was like... he saw only what was pure in me, what mattered."

Her voice softened, and for a moment, she was quiet, as if she was lost in the memory.

"There was a day," she continued, her voice almost a whisper, "when I was sitting alone, feeling the weight of everything I was carrying inside. I was crying—no one else was around. And then, I heard him. He didn't say anything at first. But there was this... soft tune. It wasn't a song, really. More like a melody that could settle your heart into stillness."

Radhika closed her eyes for a second, as if reliving the moment, the sound of it still resonating in her chest.

"It was the *basuri*," she whispered.

Anay's heart skipped. He hadn't expected her to mention it. He knew it had something to do with Madhav, but he had no idea it was such a deeply woven thread into their connection. He stayed quiet, waiting for her to continue.

"The first time I heard it; I thought I imagined it. I didn't even understand what it was. But then... every time I felt lost, sad, or unsure, the *basuri* would appear. A soft, haunting tune. Not loud, not forceful. But it would fill me up. Make me feel like there was something beyond the noise, beyond the chaos of my mind."

She looked at him then, her gaze full of something tender, something that seemed to bridge the past with the present.

"Madhav had this way of making everything make sense, even when it didn't. The sound of the *basuri* became a part of me. It wasn't just him talking to me anymore—it was *us* together. The melody told me that everything I was feeling was real. And that I wasn't alone."

She fell quiet for a moment, and Anay's chest tightened with an unfamiliar ache. It was as if he could feel the weight of her words, the history between her and Madhav, and the profound significance of that tune—the *basuri*. He didn't say anything, just let the silence surround them, hoping she would continue.

"I think..." Radhika's voice trailed off, her eyes distant again, "I think I fell in love with the way the *basuri* made me feel. Like I was a part of something grander, something timeless. It wasn't just the sound. It was the way it made me believe that I could be enough. That I could be loved... just as I was."

Anay's heart stilled in his chest. The clarity was dawning on him, piece by piece. This wasn't just a hallucination; it wasn't just a figment of her mind. Madhav—and the *basuri*—were a bridge to something deeper, something more meaningful than he'd ever realized.

Her voice broke the silence. "And that's when I knew. I knew he would always be with me."

XII
THE UNSEEN THREAD

It began in silence.

Not the dramatic silence of heartbreaks or goodbyes—but the gentle kind, the kind that arrives when two souls sit beside each other without the need to speak. That's how Radhika remembered the beginnings of her love with Madhav. A love that didn't start with fireworks or declarations. It started with stillness—like the space between two musical notes, holding more meaning than the melody itself.

It began on an evening soaked in gold. She had just returned from a long walk, the kind where your feet forget the way home but your heart doesn't. Her eyes were sore, not from crying, but from holding too much within. And then she heard it—that sound, that softness—a low, mellow tune floating in through the open balcony.

Basuri.

It wasn't a song. It wasn't even music. It was a whisper of someone who understood.

She leaned into the sound, like a moth drawn to flame, but safer. And when she reached the balcony, he was already there. Not standing or sitting—but existing. Like the moon doesn't enter the night sky, it simply *is*.

Madhav.

The boy with a smile that never asked questions. Eyes that didn't want answers. And hands that held no expectations. He wore simplicity like royalty—a loose white kurta, worn-out denim, and bare feet, always bare feet. As if the earth whispered secrets to him he didn't want to miss.

They didn't introduce themselves. They just... talked.

About clouds. About how they sometimes look like mountains. Or gods. Or old wounds.

About birds. How they migrate not just for warmth, but for reasons they probably can't explain.

About silence. And how not every silence is empty.

He would tease her gently. "You overthink, Radhi," he'd say, plucking a wildflower and tucking it behind her ear. "The stars are not gossiping about you. They're too busy dancing."

And she would laugh. Not because it was funny. But because it was safe.

There was safety in his mischief. Warmth in his mystery.

Once, she asked, "Are you real?"

He looked up from his cup of chai, eyes twinkling. "Are dreams real?"

She had no reply. Only a smile.

Their days weren't filled with plans. They were filled with pauses. Hours sitting on rooftops, watching kites flirt with the sky. Sharing kulfi on narrow lanes where time didn't chase you. Conversations with their legs dangling from the edge of the world.

She remembered one evening when she was tired—tired not physically, but with the weight of questions, expectations, timelines. She didn't want to talk. She didn't want to be fixed.

He didn't ask anything. He just sat beside her, back against the same wall. Quiet. Present.

Then, from his side, the tune began again. The basuri.

It didn't speak in words. But it said, *I'm here.* And that was enough.

Radhika didn't fall in love with Madhav like lightning hits the earth. She fell in love like petals unfolding to morning light—gradually, tenderly, without knowing when it had begun.

It wasn't about him doing things for her. It was about *being* with her.

Their love didn't have pictures. It had sensations.

The warmth of a sunbeam touching the skin. The joy of a breeze lifting your hair. The trust of shadows that always follow you.

She remembered a moment clearly. They were lying on the terrace, eyes to the sky. He said, "Do you think stars miss each other?" She turned. "Why would they?" "Because they blink. Maybe that's their way of calling out."

She had laughed. And then, quietly, held his hand.

She didn't remember when it became love. But she remembered the moment she stopped being scared of it.

Because with Madhav, love wasn't heavy. It didn't ask her to prove, perform, or protect.

It simply was.

And somewhere, deep within, Radhika knew— This love would never leave her. Because it didn't reside in the world. It resided in her.

She didn't need him to exist for it to be real.

He was her inner rhythm. The melody in her madness.

He was her basuri.

And even on the noisiest days of the world — she could still hear him play.

The story of Radhika and Madhav, if it could be called a story, did not follow chapters or plotlines. It flowed like music—sometimes soaring, sometimes silent, but always present.

In the quiet pockets of her day, when the sun draped itself lazily on her bedroom curtains or the kettle sang too soon, Madhav was there. Not with the weight of obsession, not even with the intrusion of fantasy. He was simply *there*, like warmth to her skin, like the scent of sandalwood in an empty room.

Their conversations were short sometimes—sometimes just shared glances, imagined smiles. Other times, they'd talk for what felt like hours, as if the world had agreed to pause just for them.

He'd tease her often. About the way she walked like she carried poetry in her spine. About the way she couldn't make tea without spilling a little. About how she always looked for shapes in clouds like a child.

"You're such a mess," he'd chuckle.

"And you're imaginary," she'd smirk back.

"Still more real than the people who walked out."

She would go silent at that, then smile. Because he was right.

There was a night she sat on the terrace, wrapped in a shawl, the city humming quietly below. She'd had a rough day. One of those days where the body felt too heavy to carry, and the heart too loud to ignore.

And then, he arrived. No sound, no announcement. Just presence.

"You look like a dropped diya," he said, his voice soft.

She laughed, bitter at first, but then a little lighter. "I feel like one."

And he sat beside her. Or rather, she imagined he did. But in that moment, it didn't matter.

"Want to hear a story?" he asked.

"Only if it has a happy ending."

"Then I'll have to make one up."

He told her a story of stars that used to sing to each other in the sky, until the day the moon learned to hum. And suddenly, the sky became a symphony.

"It's not about the stars," he said. "It's about the silence between them. That's where love lives."

She cried that night—not from pain, but from the relief of being understood.

And in the many evenings that followed, he'd hum a tune under his breath, sometimes playful, sometimes solemn. The tune always came from a flute.

A haunting, beautiful basuri melody. The sound never left her.

She didn't know when it became the language of her heartbeat.

She began drawing him. Not fully, never his face. Just the outlines. His silhouette against the edge of a pond. His hands in motion, as if sculpting air. The hem of a saffron robe drifting in the wind.

She imagined he loved peacocks. That he hated shoes. That he'd sit by a river and talk to birds.

She imagined, too, that he'd only ever love once.

And that once... was her.

There were moments he'd vanish. Moments where she would call out to the silence, her heart loud with longing.

And always, always, he'd return.

"I'm not real," he'd say sometimes.

"Then reality's overrated," she'd reply.

Their love wasn't loud. It didn't demand presence. It didn't crave public validation. It bloomed in hidden corners—like wildflowers that only open at dusk.

He appeared in the rain too, once. When the whole city was caught under a grey sky and umbrellas bloomed like flowers on the street. She had been walking without one, drenched, not caring, not blinking. And there he was, walking beside her.

"Trying to dissolve into the weather?" he teased.

"No," she said. "Just trying to match the ache inside."

And he took her hand. An imaginary gesture, but her pulse believed it. So did her tears, which stopped falling the moment he smiled.

He whispered poems to her in her sleep, verses she would wake up remembering like dreams she never had. About rivers that remember footsteps, about trees that weep when the wind forgets them.

She used to hum the basuri tune at traffic signals. In crowded buses. In the shower. She didn't even notice anymore—it had woven into her.

She once told him, "I think you're just a metaphor."

"And you're just a heart looking for one."

He was the silence she chose over noise. The absence that comforted her more than most presence ever could. He didn't occupy space, he occupied meaning.

She imagined him offering her marigolds. Not roses. Because marigolds looked like little suns. Because they were earthy and humble and bright.

She imagined his favorite color was the orange before sunset. That he'd always sit on rooftops. That he'd love old ghazals and mangoes and walking barefoot on cold marble floors.

In her quiet world, Madhav wasn't an escape. He was a companion to her truth.

When people spoke of love, they talked of butterflies, of late-night texts, of anniversaries and selfies and promises made under fairy lights.

Her love didn't need a timeline. Or proof. It needed silence, presence, laughter that lingered after tears, and a tune that sounded like a flute.

And so, he became the breath between her words. The shadow behind her laughter. The hum in her pauses.

A love that did not need to be touched to be felt.

A love that did not begin or end.

Just like the music of a basuri that plays long after the flautist stops.

Just like the saffron threads between moments—binding, but unseen.

He was there, quietly.

Not in the spotlight. Not in the verses of her heart's songs. But he existed—in the silences between breaths, in the thoughtful glances she gave the world, in the corner of every frame that wasn't meant to be seen.

Anay.

To Radhika, he had always been someone like a poem she never got around to reading fully, but one that lingered with a beautiful line she kept coming back to. He was her comfort, her gravity.

A consistent orbit she could depend on, even if she never looked at the sky to admire the moon.

She remembered him from their childhood, always being there—not loud, not demanding. Just there. With eyes that watched over her without intrusion. With a steadiness she never had to ask for.

He never interrupted. Not even when she vanished into her own world.

He just made sure the door was never closed.

Even when Madhav began arriving in her life—first as a thought, then as a presence, then as an impossible, infinite reality—Anay's friendship was still an armchair in the corner of the room. Always available. Never pulling her back.

She remembered once, years before marriage, when she had been sitting at the back of her college auditorium, headphones on, sketching something abstract. Anay sat beside her after the event had ended. He didn't ask what she was drawing. He didn't try to peek.

He just sat there, drinking from a paper cup and offered her the last bite of his muffin.

She never forgot that. The silence, the kindness, the lack of need.

And so, in the world where Madhav had started to grow, Anay remained her stillness.

But Madhav—oh, Madhav was everything else.

He was the breeze that knew how to tousle her hair without seeking permission. He was the laughter echoing in empty rooms. He was the boy who sat on tree branches, legs swinging mid-air, teasing her with metaphors about the rain and stars.

He was light.

He had a way of appearing when she needed him most—not in body, but in essence. Like joy that tiptoes back after a day of sadness. He teased her when she pouted, mimicked her when she was angry, and held conversations about the shape of clouds and the rhythm of pigeon wings.

She would talk to him as she watered the plants in her balcony garden.

"You're going to drown them," he would say, pointing at the drooping tulips.

"They're thirsty. Like you," she would quip.

"I only drink moonlight," he'd reply, throwing his arms up in dramatic flair.

Their world wasn't defined by space. It wasn't bound by time. It was fluid, like a poem constantly rewriting itself.

She once sat on her bed, curled up in her oversized sweater, tea untouched on the table.

"Why do you always come when I least expect you?" she whispered aloud.

Madhav, swinging an imaginary flute between his fingers, smiled. "Because you never expect joy either. But I showed up. Always."

She giggled.

And then he played it for the first time.

Not truly. Not audibly.

But she heard it—the basuri.

A melody not made of notes but of memory, warmth, and a strange ache that danced with delight.

That sound—that imagined, silent sound—became her anchor.

It was the way he played it. Not for performance. Not for admiration.

He played it like a lullaby for the earth, like a promise whispered to the wind.

In her dreams, in her moments of solitude, in her fears—she began to hear it more.

That's when she knew. That's when it began blooming—not just affection, but a love so different it didn't ask for anything in return. It was not a claim. It was a surrender.

Madhav was not hers.

He just... was.

Like an eternal companion of her soul. A keeper of her secret joy.

And in the middle of this endless warmth, the faint shadow of Anay still sat quietly at the corner—watching, listening, waiting.

But her story, for now, was only this.

A girl who fell in love with something the world could not see.

And a boy, with a flute no one else could hear, who taught her what it meant to smile even in silence.

XIII
TUNING THE HEARTSTRINGS

It began like the shy breath before a song.
Soft.
Unseen.
But inevitable.

Not with a thunderstorm of confessions,
not with the flare of sudden lightning,
but with dew on her eyelashes—
moments collecting, like petals learning how to open.

At first, she believed he was only a mirage—
a warm hallucination to cradle her loneliness.
A flicker stitched into the fabric of silence.
A name without footsteps.

But then—
he smiled.

And everything changed.

Madhav.

He was not her escape.
He was the rhythm her silences danced to.
The pause between her sighs.
The laughter blooming between her sobs.

He appeared like a memory the heart never made,
yet never forgot.

Beside her, when she stirred her morning coffee with thoughts heavier than sleep.
Perched on the swing that hadn't moved in years.
In the mirror—grinning, as he leaned over her shoulder, mimicking her expressions with absurd precision.

"That strand is rebelling again," he murmured one morning.

She frowned. "So are you."

"And yet," he winked, "you let me stay."

"That's because you're hard to hate," she admitted, brushing him off—
or pretending to.

"You make everything feel like a haiku," she once told him.

He just bowed dramatically. "Then rhyme with me, moon-girl."

And she laughed. Loud.
Freely.

The kind of laugh the world doesn't see often—because
it doesn't ask gently enough.

One night, it rained.
The kind of rain that doesn't fall—
but weeps against the windows.
She sat curled,
her tears silent, her breath slower than sleep.

And then—

A sound.
Not real. Not loud.
But inside her.
Like the earth whispering in tune.
The basuri.

Not perfect, not polished—
but aching.
As if someone was exhaling pain through melody.
A sound too gentle to be imagined,
and yet too sacred to be real.

She turned—and there he was.

Sitting on the ledge.
Barefoot.
Glowing in the hush of thunderless clouds.

"You're not supposed to be here," she whispered.

"And yet," he shrugged, "you never locked the door."

"I don't remember leaving it open."

He smiled. "You don't need to remember. You just need to feel."

She didn't argue.
She couldn't.

Because at that moment, she wasn't alone.
Not in the room.
Not in her mind.
Not in her ache.

He held her—not with hands—
but with presence.

And slowly, unknowingly, the impossible began to root.

She didn't wait for him anymore.
He didn't *arrive*—he *was*.
In the corners of sketches she didn't recall drawing.
In the breeze that turned pages she forgot she'd written.
In the echo between her words, as though he was finishing the lines
she didn't know she had begun.

He matched her silences with poetry.
Her fears with wit.
Her numbness with joy.

"You know why shadows stay close to us?" he asked once.

She shook her head.

"Because they're made of our love for light."

She didn't answer.
She didn't need to.
Because the ache in her chest had already been understood.

And then it happened.

Not a plunge.
Not a leap.
But it is blooming.

She looked around one day and realized—
she had been in love all along.

There was no *beginning*.
Just the quiet becoming something inevitable.

And Madhav—he stopped teasing that day.
Only for a moment.

He looked at her as if she were a song finally sung.

"You heard it, didn't you?" he asked.

"Heard what?"

"The music inside you. The one I was only echoing."

And she did.
She heard it everywhere now.
In the fluttering of curtains.
In the pauses between birdsongs.
In the soft hiccup of her own heartbeat.

It was love.

Not a love that needed proof.
Or plans.
Or permanence.

But a love made of air and ache.
Of joy and silence.
Of someone who existed only when she closed her eyes—
yet felt more real than any hand she had ever held.

Madhav.

Her unseen companion.
Her midnight muse.
Her flute-bearer of serenity.

She was his.

Completely.
Irrevocably.

Even if the world could never see him.

Even if her lips would never speak of him aloud.

Even if her heart had to hum its lullabies alone.

He was hers—
and she, his.

Not in the ways books would call love.

But in the stillness where no one watches—
and everything becomes true.

The room, bathed in the fading light of a late
afternoon, felt different now. Radhika had finished her

story, the air still heavy with the presence of Madhav—more real in the quiet than he ever was in the spoken word. Anay sat, his mind a whirlwind, yet his eyes were fixed on Radhika. She was the only thing solid in this sea of emotions and ideas.

But it wasn't just her anymore.

It was him too.

Madhav.

And that name, that presence, continued to echo in the spaces between them.

"Okay," Anay said after a pause, the words slipping out with an unexpected sense of purpose. "I want to try something."

Radhika, who had been gazing out the window, turning her thoughts into the last tendrils of the day's sunlight, turned to look at him. "Try something? What now?"

A small smile crept across his face. It was half-hopeful, half-awkward—like someone fumbling for a key but certain it would unlock something that mattered. "The flute," he said, as though it was the most natural thing in the world. "Madhav... he plays it, right? I want to learn."

Radhika's lips quirked into a teasing smile almost immediately. "Oh, this should be good," she said, a spark of mischief in her eyes. "Do you really think you can just pick up a flute and *become* Madhav? You've seen him play, right? It's not as easy as it looks. The breath, the rhythm, the soul of it..."

"I know," Anay interrupted, holding up his hand. "I'm not trying to be him. But I want to try. I want to learn what that sound means. The way he makes it... I think I can do it. For you."

Radhika raised an eyebrow, her expression playful. "For me, huh? You really think you can learn it? Because, you know, you're already pretty terrible at blowing out birthday candles."

Anay chuckled, the playful tension in the air thickening. "That was one time, and that cake was too big."

"Well, the flute's definitely smaller," Radhika teased. "But the sound it makes? That's a whole other level." She crossed her arms. "I'm telling you, you won't be able to do it. There's a reason Madhav plays it, and not everyone gets to. There's something... special about it."

Anay leaned forward, his voice dropping, playful but earnest. "You're underestimating me."

Radhika's eyes sparkled with amusement as she leaned back into the chair, crossing one leg over the other. "You think you can master the flute and suddenly become this magical being? Like him?" she teased.

"I'll master it," Anay said confidently, though inside, he felt the flutter of uncertainty in his chest. He wasn't a musician. But for her, for this love that had been an echo in her heart, he was ready to try. To be something more.

"Alright," Radhika finally relented, uncrossing her arms. "I'll help you... but don't expect me to go easy on you."

Anay grinned. "Deal."

Radhika stood up and walked toward the corner of the room, where an old flute lay. It was worn, the wood smooth from years of use, but the memories it held—those seemed to echo louder than anything physical. She picked it up and looked at it for a moment, her fingers brushing the cool surface.

Anay sat, watching her with intent eyes. "So... where do we start?"

She raised the flute to her lips, then lowered it again, as if considering his question. "The flute isn't just about the sound. It's about *breathing* into it. About letting the air become a part of the music. If you're going to try, you have to understand that first."

"Breathing," Anay murmured. "The breath that Madhav makes sound."

Radhika nodded, her expression softening a little. "Yes. You can't make the music if you're holding your breath. It has to flow through you."

She handed the flute to him, but Anay hesitated. His fingers closed around it gently, the sensation unfamiliar. Holding it, he felt the weight of something more than just wood in his hands. It was the weight of trust. The weight of trying to become something he wasn't—but something he was willing to grow into.

"Okay, now you'll blow into it," Radhika instructed. "But don't try to force it. It's not about power; it's about release. It's about letting yourself be vulnerable to the air."

Anay closed his eyes for a moment, taking a deep breath, and then he pressed the flute to his lips. The first attempt was a failure—a soft puff of air with no sound. He grimaced. "See? I told you. I can't do it."

Radhika laughed, her voice light and teasing. "Don't give up that quickly. You're just not letting the air *flow*." She leaned in, her eyes meeting his with a playful intensity. "Remember, it's not about making a sound. It's about learning the *silence* first. The music will come after."

"Silence first?" Anay raised an eyebrow.

"Exactly," she said, the teasing fading into something deeper. "You have to understand the stillness before you can make noise."

Anay exhaled deeply and tried again. He focused, trying to clear his mind of everything—of Madhav, of the expectation, of the desire to impress. Just breathe.

The second time, a faint sound escaped the flute. It was not the music he had imagined. But it was something. And that small something made him smile.

Radhika's eyes softened. "See? You're getting it."

"I'm trying," Anay admitted. He took another breath, this time deeper, slower.

The flute responded, and a sound—more than a note, less than a song—filled the room.

"Not bad for a first try," Radhika said, her tone light but with a proud edge.

Anay chuckled, wiping a bead of sweat from his forehead. "Yeah, well, I'm no Madhav. But I'll keep at it."

Radhika stood beside him, her eyes narrowing in mock contemplation. "You know," she said slowly, "there's something about the way Madhav plays that's different. It's not just the notes. It's the way the air carries his feelings... his heart."

Anay looked at her, a sudden understanding stirring in his chest. "You've always said his music made you feel alive," he murmured. "What do you feel when he plays?"

Radhika's gaze softened as she leaned against the table, her eyes distant, like she was hearing the echoes of him somewhere deep inside her. "I feel like... like he's part of the world. The way the wind is. Invisible, yet everywhere. And somehow... always near."

Anay nodded slowly, the weight of her words pressing into him. He wanted to understand this. To understand *her*.

And so, with that promise in his heart, he continued to breathe into the flute. Slowly, carefully, like learning to listen to a melody that wasn't his own—but one he needed to understand, just for her.

XIV
Echoes of a Flute's Breath

The evening was quiet, the last vestiges of daylight fading behind the city's skyline. Radhika sat on the balcony, a gentle breeze brushing through her hair, as if it, too, was part of her reverie. Anay sat opposite her, his presence unobtrusive but ever steady. He could see the slight curve of her lips, the way her eyes held a story yet to be told. The air between them hummed with a silent understanding.

She took a slow breath and, without turning to him, began. "There was no grand moment between Madhav and me. No dramatic confession, no carefully planned words." She paused, a small smile playing at her lips. "It was more like... a song that started without us realizing it. A melody that was always there, just waiting for us to hear it."

Anay leaned in, intrigued, waiting for her to continue. "Tell me," he encouraged softly, his voice almost a whisper.

Radhika's gaze drifted to the horizon, her fingers tracing the rim of her coffee cup as she spoke. Her voice, as always, held that quiet depth, like a song that didn't need loud notes to be heard.

"It started with the silence," she began, her words flowing like a stream. "You know, the kind of silence that speaks without saying anything. The kind that makes your heart understand things before your mind does."

She paused, lost in her thoughts for a moment. Anay waited. The silence between them wasn't awkward; it was simply the space where words were not needed.

"It was in the small things first. The way he would just *be* there," Radhika continued, her fingers brushing against the edge of the balcony. "Not physically, but in ways that didn't need an explanation. He was like the wind—soft, fleeting, but constant. At first, I thought it was just my imagination, my mind playing tricks on me, making up stories."

She smiled softly at the thought.

Madhav's voice suddenly echoed in her memory, as clear as if he were standing right beside her. "*You're always imagining things, Radhika. Maybe you should imagine me properly, and not just as a shadow.*"

Radhika chuckled at the memory, shaking her head. "He always had a way of teasing me, you know? He used to say that I had a terrible imagination. But really, it was him who was the one to fill the spaces between my thoughts."

Anay smiled, leaning back in his chair, listening intently, yet not interrupting.

Radhika continued, her voice growing more tender as she relived the moments. "*How can someone be so real, and yet feel like a dream?*" she whispered, remembering how Madhav would always ask her these kinds of questions. "*Maybe you're just a dream that I've been waiting to wake up from,*" she remembered saying to him once.

Madhav's voice responded in her mind, as if it were a part of the very air around them. "*Then let's never wake up,*" he'd answered, with that quiet certainty that only he had. "*Let's stay in this dream together, where there's no need for waking up, no need for anything else.*"

Radhika's eyes fluttered closed for a moment, as if feeling his presence there beside her, just for a heartbeat.

Anay watched her closely, feeling the weight of her words. He couldn't fully understand it—not yet—but there was something undeniably beautiful about the way Radhika spoke of Madhav. It wasn't loud, it wasn't demanding. It was simply the truth of her heart, unfolding quietly.

She opened her eyes again and continued, her voice soft and far away. "There was this one night, after it had rained. The kind of rain that you could feel in your bones, the kind that made the world quiet. I had been sitting by the window, just staring out at the city lights, when I heard it. I wasn't sure if I'd really heard it or if it was just in my mind. But it came through—"*the basuri.*""

Her smile was distant, but her voice held a warmth. "I knew it was him. I didn't need to look, didn't need to question. I could feel him with me in the sound of that flute."

Anay stayed still, trying to piece together the pieces of this love—this quiet, magical love that Radhika shared with someone who existed in the silence between them. "What did it feel like?" he asked softly, his words barely breaking the stillness.

Radhika's smile deepened, as if she were reliving the memory. "It was the kind of sound that filled the spaces in my chest. It was like a comfort I didn't even know I needed. Soft, like the wind carrying a song. The kind that settles deep inside you, like a seed that knows it will bloom. The basuri. It wasn't perfect, Anay. It wasn't rehearsed. But it was real. And it made me realize that I wasn't alone. That somehow, this was enough."

She paused for a moment, her voice thick with emotion. "*I could feel his presence in every note, every breath of the music.*"

Anay leaned forward, sensing the shift in her energy. "That night..." he said slowly, trying to understand, "What happened that night?"

Radhika smiled softly, her eyes closing for just a moment as she conjured the memory. "That night, I realized something important. It wasn't the big moments, the declarations, the promises. It was the silence between us. The way we existed together without needing to fill the space with anything. We didn't need words, Anay. We only needed each other, in the quiet, in the sound of the basuri, and in the spaces where love didn't need to be spoken aloud."

Anay's chest tightened as he listened. Her words were profound in their simplicity. There was no need for grand gestures when love existed in the small things. In the spaces between, in the moments that felt like they could slip away unnoticed, but were the ones that mattered most.

"Was that when you realized you loved him?" Anay asked, his voice soft, almost a whisper.

Radhika nodded slowly; her smile almost imperceptible. "Yes," she said, her voice barely a breath. "At that moment, when I heard the basuri, I didn't need anything else. I just knew. I was in love. Not with the idea of him. Not with the future we could have. But with him. As he was. As he is. Without asking for more."

Her words lingered in the air between them. There was no need for anything else. It was simply the truth of her heart, spoken softly and truthfully.

Anay felt the weight of her words, the quiet beauty of her love for Madhav. He didn't need to understand everything, but he understood this much—there was a depth to Radhika's heart, a love that needed no explanation, no grand gesture. It was just there, in the silence, in the music, in the presence of two souls who didn't need to ask for anything more than what they already had.

Radhika's eyes met Anay's, a small but knowing smile on her lips. "This," she whispered, "was love. Quiet. Unspoken. But completely, utterly real."

Anay sat there, a few moments of silence hanging in the air after Radhika's words had settled. The balcony, which had felt like a quiet space of conversation, now felt like the weight of a thousand thoughts pressing in. Radhika, with her tender smile and poetic words, had unfolded a love so deep, so personal, that he almost felt like an intruder to it.

He knew it was not his place to feel this way. But, in that moment, he couldn't help it.

The weight of what Radhika had shared—Madhav's music, the way he existed in her world with such subtle, unspoken devotion—made Anay feel small. Not in a way that would break him, no. But in a way that reminded him of how far he had yet to go.

Radhika was telling him this story, her heart laid bare in the delicate melody of her words. And Anay could feel the echoes of that love—of Madhav's silent presence, the music of the flute, the way he had made her feel seen even without being there.

And now, here he was, sitting across from her, just... Anay.

Madhav was more than a name. He was a spirit, a melody, a rhythm. The kind of presence that was irreplaceable.

Anay sighed quietly as Radhika, blissfully unaware of the weight pressing on his chest, smiled, her eyes soft as she finished her tale. He had to pull himself together, but it wasn't easy. The realization hit him in waves, pulling at him like an undercurrent in the ocean—he was trying to become something he could never be.

The flute. The sound of it. He had to learn. He had to be that same force for Radhika, somehow, even if he couldn't match what Madhav was to her.

That night, after Radhika had returned to her home, Anay found himself alone in his room. The flute sat there in front of him, silent, its hollow body still as the weight of its purpose stared him down.

He reached out and held it carefully, feeling its smooth surface in his hands. It was foreign to him. He wasn't sure where to begin, where to place his fingers, how to breathe through it. Everything about this felt alien, and yet it felt necessary.

With a deep breath, Anay pressed the flute to his lips.

The first note came out awkwardly, sharp and wrong, as if the instrument itself was reluctant to make sound. His fingers trembled on the holes, the air coming out unevenly. It was nothing like what Madhav's music would have been. It was clumsy and incomplete, and the sound felt harsh—nothing but noise, a far cry from the music that had filled Radhika's heart.

He exhaled sharply, setting the flute down. His hands were shaking now. Was he really this bad? Was he even capable of learning this?

The memory of Radhika's smile when she had mentioned Madhav's music, the way her voice had softened, the warmth in her eyes as she spoke of him... it all felt like a distant dream, something he could never touch. How could he even begin to compete with that kind of love? With that kind of connection?

But he wasn't here to compete. He was here to learn. To become something for her, for Radhika, who needed him in ways he couldn't even articulate. He had made a promise to himself. He couldn't falter now.

Anay closed his eyes, the weight of his feelings pressing in on him again. He missed the ease with which Madhav had become a part of Radhika's life. Madhav had made her feel whole without doing anything grand. His music, his presence, had filled the spaces in her soul. And here Anay was, trying to fill those same spaces, but fumbling with something as simple as a flute.

But in that fumbling, he felt something raw stir within him. A deep ache, a longing to be that person for her. Not just a friend. Not just the man who would protect her. But someone who could make her feel the way Madhav had made her feel—seen, heard, loved in a way that was quiet but unwavering.

He took a deep breath, resting the flute back to his lips, this time with a steadier hand. He focused on the sound, trying again.

The second note was better. Not perfect, but clearer. Still far from the beautiful, aching music Madhav had played for Radhika, but it was something.

Anay pressed his fingers down more gently, concentrating on the breath. The sound was still tentative, but it felt like he was reaching for something deeper. His own pain—his confusion, his inadequacy—flowed into the music, creating a soft, fragile rhythm that, though imperfect, carried with it the hope that he could become more.

As he played, he thought of Radhika, her smile, the way she had looked at him earlier that evening. She had trusted him with her story. She had opened her heart, and now he was opening his, too. Even if he could never truly replicate the presence of Madhav, maybe, just maybe, he could offer her something of his own. Something real.

The music lingered in the air. Not perfect, not polished, but raw and true. It wasn't the melody of a flute player with years of experience. It was the sound of a man learning, stumbling through the dark, trying to find a way to become what he believed she deserved.

And though he felt the weight of the task ahead, he couldn't help but believe that this—the struggle, the effort—was part of the journey. Maybe that was enough. Maybe, in time, the sound would grow into something more beautiful. Something that would remind her of the way he felt about her.

But for now, Anay played, lost in the rhythm of his own broken melody, knowing that it was the only way he could truly begin.

Anay sat on the edge of the bed, the flute resting on his lap. His fingers still ached from playing, and though the melody had become smoother with practice, it wasn't enough. He wasn't sure what he was chasing anymore—was it just the music? Or was it something deeper, something hidden behind the notes, that he needed to understand?

He thought about Radhika, and the story she had shared. Madhav's music, his presence, the way he had slipped into her world like a breeze she never saw coming, and yet somehow felt like home. But there was one thing that lingered in Anay's mind—one thing that had been gnawing at him since Radhika's narrative had unfolded: *Why Madhav?*

It wasn't just that she had created him. It wasn't just that she had made him a part of her life. Anay understood that love, and particularly the love Radhika had for Madhav, was more than just a simple connection. It was something intangible, something wrapped in melodies and shadows. But what inspired him? What made him *real* for her?

What was the reason she had chosen to weave him into the fabric of her soul?

Anay had spent so much time trying to be like Madhav in the simplest, most technical sense—learning the flute, trying to understand the music, hoping that somehow, he would find his way into Radhika's heart by replicating what Madhav had done.

But this wasn't about notes or breath or technique. It was about *why* Madhav existed in the first place.

He had to know.

In the stillness of the room, Anay stared at the flute. He could feel the weight of the question pressing against his chest, thick like the silence that filled the space. But no answers were coming. It felt like there was something just beyond his reach, a veil over the truth, and he couldn't seem to peel it away.

He needed to ask her.

The thought came like a spark, sudden and undeniable. He could ask her—he could sit down and have this conversation, delve deeper into the reasons why Madhav had appeared in her mind. Radhika had already shared so much with him, and had trusted him with her heart. But this was different. This was a question that hung in the air, waiting to be answered. And yet, he hesitated.

He thought of how Radhika's eyes had sparkled when she spoke of Madhav—how she had described him as someone who filled the spaces in her life with music. But what did she mean by that? What was the deeper meaning? Why had she crafted him from the fabric of her imagination, and why had he become such an integral part of her? Anay couldn't ignore the nagging question any longer.

He couldn't keep playing this game of mimicry without understanding. He had to know the root, the origin of it all.

Suddenly, the realization hit him. Maybe it wasn't just about Madhav at all. Maybe the answer lay within Radhika herself. *Why did she need him?*

And the more he thought about it, the more he began to understand that this question wasn't just about the creation of Madhav—it was about Radhika's own need for him. Her love, her connection to him, the way she had woven him into her world like a melody that could never fade, was a question that only she could answer.

But then, a new thought entered his mind—a quiet, unsettling thought. What if the answer wasn't something she could share? What if the reason Madhav existed in her mind was something even Radhika didn't fully understand herself? What if this was more than just a need for comfort, more than just a fantasy—what if it was something that stretched beyond her consciousness?

It was then that Anay realized how little he truly understood her. Madhav, as much as he wanted to replicate him, as much as he wanted to *be* him for her, was more than just a figure to be imitated. He was a part of her, a piece of her soul that he couldn't touch—not yet.

His heart tightened, the thought lingering like a shadow. He couldn't deny it. As much as he had learned to play the flute and had tried to understand Radhika through her stories, there was a depth to her love for Madhav that he could never fully reach. Not until she was ready to show him.

But the question remained: *What had inspired him?*

Anay stood up, the flute resting loosely in his hands. He needed to know. And the next time they spoke, he would ask her. He would push past his fears, his insecurities, and get to the heart of the matter.

But even as he made that decision, a quiet voice in the back of his mind whispered:

What if the answer was something he wasn't prepared to hear?

It was a question he couldn't ignore.

Anay's breath caught in his throat. He looked at the flute in his hands, the instrument that had become a symbol of his attempts to bridge the gap between himself and the world Radhika shared with Madhav. The silence was heavy now, the air thick with unspoken thoughts.

His eyes flicked to the door, where Radhika's absence felt like a presence in itself.

What if she had already given him the answer, but he hadn't seen it yet?

He closed his eyes, feeling the weight of the question on his heart. There was no easy answer. No clear path forward. All he could do now was wait—wait for the right moment, the right words, the right understanding to come to him.

But for now, the uncertainty was all-consuming. And as Anay sat back down, picking up the flute once more, he knew that what lay ahead was more than just learning music. It was about uncovering truths that were hidden beneath the surface—truths that could either bring him closer to Radhika or shatter the fragile thread they had built.

The melody played on, soft and unsure, as the question echoed in his mind.

And the story—Radhika's story, Madhav's story—remained suspended in the silence between the notes.

XV
MELODIES IN THE STORM

The morning was quiet in a way that didn't demand silence—it invited it. The kind of hush that lets the smallest sounds bloom.

Anay sat cross-legged on the terrace floor, the city below unaware of the symphony building in a corner of its sky. The sun hadn't climbed fully yet, and the wind still carried the crisp calmness of dawn. A mug of untouched coffee sat beside him, cold now, long forgotten.

In his hands rested the wooden flute. Smooth, light, yet full of secrets.

His fingers trembled—not with fear, but reverence.

He brought it to his lips. Closed his eyes. Took a breath.

"Sa..."

The note came out like a whisper lost in a dream. He paused. Adjusted his fingers.

"Re…"

This one cracked a little. Off-key. Imperfect. But sincere.

Each note wasn't just a sound; it was an emotion. A confession. A hope.

He didn't want to play music. He wanted to understand her music. Her world. Her rhythm.

Unbeknownst to him, behind the sheer curtain of the open window, Radhika watched.

Wrapped in the soft folds of a cotton shawl, her eyes stayed fixed on him—not critically, not expectantly, but gently… like watching a flower try to bloom in the off-season.

She didn't smile. She didn't cry. She just listened.

And the notes he struggled to produce seemed to echo within her in strange ways—almost as if they were memories trying to remember themselves.

Anay tried again.

"Ga…"

Still not right. But it didn't matter.

Because he was there. Breathing into a flute. Not to impress. Not to master. But to become fluent in her language.

A language of pauses. Of silences. Of sounds that came from the soul and not the throat.

With every breath he gave the basuri, it gave something back—fragile, flawed, but alive.

The flute rested between his fingers like it had been waiting to come home.

There was a moment—between *Ga* and *Ma*, somewhere in the breath between two notes—where Anay paused. And in that pause, something shifted. Something ancient. Something that didn't belong to the logic of now.

He adjusted his posture—not consciously, but instinctively. Like his spine remembered a rhythm from another time. His fingers moved—not perfectly, not expertly—but with an ease that felt eerily familiar.

As if they were not learning.

But remembering.

Like he had played this before. Not in this lifetime, not with this body... but somewhere, somehow, in a time memory had forgotten, his soul had once held this wooden wind and whispered music into the world.

The notes began to shape themselves.

Still raw. Still fragile.

But no longer strangers to his breath.

They came out like lost children finding their way home—stumbling, falling, but with joy in their steps.

Sa... Re... Ga... Ma... Pa...

He wasn't just playing now. He was becoming something.

He was speaking.

Not in words, but in ache. In longing. In silent promises made without a single sound.

The flute had stopped being an instrument. It had become a bridge.

Between him and something infinite.

Between him and her.

Up above, Radhika hadn't moved.

She was still behind the window, her shawl now wrapped tighter, but not from cold. From awe.

She watched not a man trying to play her music, but a soul finding its own way into it. Into her.

There was a strange comfort in it. Like seeing someone walk barefoot into a temple, not because they were told to, but because their steps knew to.

The wind carried the tune he was learning—soft and incomplete—like a prayer still being written.

But it was enough.

Enough for the morning to feel sacred.

Enough for Radhika's gaze to soften just a little more.

Enough for Anay to feel, for the first time, not like an outsider in her world... but like a note in her song.

Radhika's eyes lingered on Anay as the soft notes of the basuri continued to hum through the air, each sound intertwining with the silence of the room. She sat back, leaning against the edge of the window, her hands folded tightly in her lap as her heart began to race, albeit in a quiet, steady rhythm.

Sa, Re, Ga...

The music was uneven, as expected. But there was something in it—something more than mere effort. It was genuine, it was real. The sound of his breath, each exhaled note, was as much an expression of his heart as it was an attempt to play the flute.

She couldn't help but watch him, though she knew he wouldn't notice her. His back was turned to her as he practiced, lost in his pursuit of learning something that felt so intimately tied to her. It was strange, watching him like this, with that quiet determination, the furrow in his brow that came with each failed attempt. But what haunted her was the sudden understanding of how deeply he cared for her. How much he was willing to do for her.

And that's when the guilt struck her.

The flute played on, but Radhika felt the walls of her chest tighten. Her eyes closed for a moment, trying to push the rising anxiety down. This wasn't what she had expected. She had known that Anay cared about her deeply, but this? This was beyond anything she had anticipated.

He was playing for her. For the connection they had yet to build, for the space that she had, time and again, kept locked away in the farthest corners of her heart. The music was his way of reaching her, of proving that he was willing to do whatever it took to meet her where she was.

But what did that mean for her?

A single breath escaped her lips, shaky and uncertain. She stood, pacing the length of the room, as the music swirled around her, intensifying the turmoil inside her. She had given him something he didn't deserve—a promise she had never meant to make.

When did it happen? When had she allowed him to become a part of her heart? She had tried so hard to keep him at a distance, to protect herself from the inevitable pain that would come with opening up to him. But now... Now, she had created a mess she didn't know how to untangle.

Was this fair to him?

That thought gnawed at her relentlessly. She had always been cautious about what she gave to others, guarding her heart with an iron fist. But with Anay, it had been so easy to slip. So easy to let him in, even when she hadn't wanted to. Even when she had fought so hard to keep her emotions locked away.

He had become so much to her in ways she hadn't been prepared for. His presence in her life, the way he listened without asking too much, the way he cared without demanding. He was there for her in ways that nobody had ever been before, and it felt... comfortable. It felt safe.

But that comfort was suffocating her now. It wasn't supposed to be this way. She wasn't supposed to be the one to make him feel like he could save her.

The guilt continued to weigh on her chest, as the music floated toward her ears. Every note felt like an accusation, reminding her of the promise she hadn't kept.

Her heart tightened as the weight of it all became unbearable.

What had she done?

Had she, in her own confusion, led him to believe that she was capable of feeling something real for him? That she could ever feel the same way he did for her? She had been playing a game with herself—pretending that her connection with Anay could be something simple, something pure, without realizing that it was evolving into something deeper.

And the truth hit her hard: she had allowed herself to build something she wasn't sure she could carry.

Radhika glanced back at Anay, who was still lost in the music, oblivious to the storm brewing inside her. The guilt swelled again, sharper this time.

She could see the hope in his eyes, the quiet belief that, maybe, somehow, she could come to care for him in the way he cared for her.

And she could feel herself pulling away from that hope.

How could I give him this hope, when I know it's not real?

The flute's melody became quieter, fading into the background as she began to retreat into her thoughts. She wasn't sure if she could ever give Anay what he truly deserved. Not while Madhav was still woven so deeply into the fabric of her heart. Not when her mind kept pulling her back to the love that wasn't real, the love she had built as a fortress for herself, to protect her from the world.

Was this fair?

To herself, to Anay, to the love that he so clearly sought from her?

Her heart ached at the thought. She wasn't ready to give him the answers he was asking for, because in doing so, she would have to give him pieces of her heart she wasn't sure she could ever part with.

A soft, almost imperceptible sigh escaped her lips as she turned back toward the window.

She didn't know how to stop this. To stop him. To stop herself.

The guilt crept in, sleeping deeper with every note of the basuri that reached her ears. She had opened a door she didn't know how to close.

And now, she had to figure out how to deal with the consequences.

The room was silent again, save for the distant sound of the flute, which had now become so familiar it felt like the rhythm of her own heartbeat. Radhika sat motionless, her thoughts swirling around her like a storm that had no name, only the weight of its arrival.

She closed her eyes, but the silence only intensified the noise inside her. It was as if the very air around her was pressing in, suffocating her, and yet, she felt a strange, familiar calmness begin to take root.

A whisper.

Not a sound. Not a voice, but a feeling. A presence.

You're not alone.

Her chest tightened as she felt a light pressure against her ribs. It was him. She knew it without question.

The air around her shifted, warm and intimate, as though the room itself had folded to accommodate him. And there, standing in the corner of her mind, was Madhav.

She hadn't heard him in so long. The real Madhav—the one who always seemed to know exactly what to say, the one who made her feel understood in a way no one else could. He was there now, his presence so strong that it almost felt like he was standing beside her. She didn't need to see him to feel him. He was always there, like the invisible thread connecting them even when the world tried to pull them apart.

His voice, quiet and steady, resonated in her mind, not as an audible sound, but as a gentle whisper that caressed her thoughts.

"Why do you look so lost, Radha? You're searching for something you already have."

She could feel his gaze on her, even though his form was nowhere to be seen. He wasn't pressing her, but rather, offering her a safe space to just be. The world outside was so loud, so frantic with its expectations and its rules. But Madhav—Madhav had never asked her to be anything but herself. He had never asked her to choose a side in the battle of the world. He had simply allowed her to be free.

Radhika squeezed her eyes shut tighter, the pain of her confusion clawing at her chest. She could feel the world spinning around her, the weight of her thoughts beginning to drown her. She couldn't find the answers. She couldn't make sense of any of it. And yet, when Madhav spoke, it felt like everything else faded into the background.

"You are not broken. You never were. You are exactly who you are supposed to be, Radha."

The words washed over her like a balm. She felt the tension in her body release, but it was fleeting, like the calm before a storm.

For a brief moment, everything felt right. Everything felt... safe.

But then, as if the words themselves had triggered it, her head began to ache. The familiar dizziness returned, the weight of her thoughts growing heavier. She pressed her hands to her temples, trying to push away the fog that was clouding her mind.

"Don't fight it." Madhav's voice was a soft caress, as though he were beside her, holding her in a way that only he could. *"You do not have to make sense to anyone. You do not have to be anything for anyone. Not even for yourself, Radha. Just be."*

The words were soothing, yes, but the ache in her head was growing worse. It was as though the fog had turned into something more tangible, pressing down on her thoughts, pushing her further into the depths of a world that was becoming more and more difficult to navigate.

Her heart began to race. The room seemed to close in on her, but in the midst of the panic, there was still his presence, still that comforting whisper, like a lifeline.

"Come to me." The words were almost a command now, but they didn't feel forceful. They felt like an invitation—a gentle call, not from the world, but from a place beyond it. *"You don't have to carry all of this alone. Let go of your burden. Come, and I will take it away."*

Her breath hitched as she stood, as if drawn by an invisible force. The room spun as she moved towards the window, her feet light but unsure, like she was walking through a dream. Outside, the world was still, but her mind was a storm.

Come to me.

The voice repeated, growing stronger, like a beacon in the fog.

And for a moment, she let go. Let go of the world, of the questions, of the confusion. She stepped into the quiet, the stillness, and as she did, the pain in her head subsided, just a little. She could still feel the weight of it, but it was muted now, as though Madhav's presence had softened its edges.

"I'm here." His voice was a soft, soothing melody, like a lullaby.

And for that brief, fragile moment, Radhika felt safe. As though the chaos of the world could not reach her, not as long as he was here. But she knew, too, that this was fleeting. She knew that the storm inside her wasn't going to end. It was only just beginning.

But she would stay in this moment for as long as she could. She would hold onto this peace, this love, even if it was only temporary.

"You will always find me, Radha." Madhav's voice was so sure, so unwavering. *"Even when you can't see me, I will always be here. In your heart, in your soul. I will never leave you."*

She smiled softly, even as the heaviness in her chest returned. He was right. She would never be alone.

And as she stood there, her hands resting lightly against the window, she could almost hear the faintest sound of the flute in the distance—so soft, so distant, but so full of love. She closed her eyes and let it wash over her, letting the music soothe her, even as the world around her became harder to understand.

But in the quiet, beneath the surface of it all, there was a shift—a subtle warning that Radhika could not ignore. It was in the way her thoughts felt jagged, disconnected, like she was losing control of the very fabric of her mind. The dizziness was no longer just physical. It was mental. The world around her seemed to shimmer and blur, like she was standing on the edge of something—something she couldn't see, but felt deep within her soul.

She didn't know if she could hold on much longer. But for now, Madhav's presence was all that kept her grounded. And she clung to it like a lifeline.

The chapter ended with Radhika standing by the window, her mind tangled in the fog of her thoughts, but her heart, for a moment, at peace.

And Madhav's promise echoed softly in her mind: *"I will never leave you."*

The rain had come with fury. The sky, once serene and bright, now twisted with an ominous shade of grey. As the wind howled, it carried with it a sense of wildness—of something unhinged, something untamable. The storm roared, as if nature itself had mirrored the turbulence inside Anay's heart. Thunder clapped like the universe had cracked open its sky to express its own rage. The air was thick, saturated, heavy with the promise of something yet to come.

And yet, amidst all the chaos, the house stood quiet. The walls cradled the sound of the rain as if they, too, were keeping a secret.

Anay stood in the hallway, feeling the storm pulse in his veins. He had practiced until his fingers ached, until his soul had become a part of the music. But the moment he left the room, the moment he sought out Radhika, everything shifted. It wasn't just the physical distance that separated them. No, it was something much deeper—a gap that had always existed, one that he could never cross, no matter how much he tried.

The closer he came to her, the stronger the storm seemed to grow. Each step felt like an assault on his own resolve, like the universe was conspiring to tear him apart.

He arrived at the door, the soft light of the room spilling out into the hallway, illuminating the shadows that clung to his body. Inside, Radhika sat by the window, her gaze fixed outward, her face softened by the quiet hum of a world she inhabited all her own. She didn't see him. Her eyes were locked onto something beyond the glass, a place where only Madhav seemed to exist.

He stood frozen, watching her from the doorway. The rain was coming down harder now, drumming violently against the windows. But it was not the rain that caught his attention. It was the stillness of Radhika, the softness of her expression, the way she seemed to float in a place he could never follow. She was distant, far away—lost in her own thoughts, in her own world. She wasn't here with him. She was elsewhere.

Anay's heart twisted. The ache that had started as a subtle discomfort now gnawed at him, deep and relentless. He watched her, unable to move, unable to break the invisible barrier that separated them. The air around him crackled with an electric tension, a tension that surged through him like the building storm. He was drawn to her, yes, but something stopped him. A sudden clarity gripped his heart—a realization that he could never be the one to fill the space that Madhav occupied in her mind.

He took a slow step forward, his heart beating faster, louder. He wasn't ready to confront it yet. He wasn't ready to face the pain of seeing her so absorbed in someone else, someone she had created. His feet faltered, and with a strangled breath, he stopped. The storm outside seemed to recognize his struggle, the thunder shaking the very ground beneath his feet, and the wind howling through the cracks in the walls.

He couldn't be the one to disrupt her peace. He couldn't take her away from the solace she found in Madhav. It wasn't his place.

Anay turned slowly, walking away from the door, as if retreating from an invisible battlefield. The music inside him swelled—a deep, aching need to release everything that had been pent up inside him. He reached for his basuri, fingers trembling as he grasped it with both hands. There was no thought in his mind, no hesitation in his movement. The pain, the longing, the confusion—everything poured into the music.

His lips met the flute, and without another thought, he played.

The notes came with ease, smoother than they ever had before. The raag rang out—pure, unyielding, and haunting. But this time, there was something new. The sorrow was sharper. The grief was deeper. It wasn't just music—it was everything. His heart wrenched with every note, each breath a plea to be heard, to be understood. The music felt like a storm inside of him, matching the fury of the weather outside. The sound wrapped around him, pulling him deeper into his own despair, his own heartache.

With each note, he poured his soul into the instrument. His sorrow danced through the air, twined with his anger, his frustration, and his sadness. He had never played like this before. It was as if the basuri had become an extension of himself, an extension of his pain, an extension of his broken heart.

As the storm outside intensified, so did the music. The wind slammed against the windows, the thunder cracked like the heavens themselves were tearing apart, but still, Anay played. The raag grew louder, more resonant, as if it had taken on a life of its own. His hands moved faster, the notes sharper, each one cascading from him like a rush of water, unable to stop, unable to hold back. It was the sound of his soul breaking, of his heart unraveling, of his love that would never be returned. He played with everything he had—his grief, his anger, his disappointment, all pouring out in the storm's rhythm.

The rain lashed harder against the windows, matching the intensity of his sorrow, the vibrations of his music intertwining with the storm's chaos. It was like they were one. Like he and the storm were bound in their rage, their fury, their helplessness.

Inside the room, Radhika was unaware of the storm, both outside and within Anay. She sat still, her head resting against the cool glass of the window, her thoughts lost in a world only she could understand. Her fingers rested gently on the edge of the sill, as if feeling the presence of something far beyond her.

In the depth of her mind, she was with Madhav—he Madhav. And there, in that world, she found a peace that eluded her in reality. Her eyes fluttered closed, the tension in her body dissipating as she drifted into sleep, unaware of the passage of time.

In her dreams, she found herself in Madhav's embrace, safe and cherished. It was the same as it had always been—the warmth of his arms surrounding her, the soft murmur of his voice, the quiet peace that settled in her chest. For a moment, she was untouchable, invincible. But what she didn't realize was that as she fell asleep, her body had unconsciously shifted closer to the window. She had drifted into sleep, not realizing that she wasn't in Madhav's arms at all. She was alone.

Anay's music, meanwhile, grew louder, more frantic. His emotions were now a whirlwind, his breath ragged, as though he was fighting against some unseen force. The raag was no longer just a melody—it was an echo of his pain, his desire to be more, to be the one who could make her feel loved in the way he could never express.

But that was the truth, wasn't it? He couldn't be Madhav. He could never be the one to offer her the love she had woven into the fabric of her mind. And yet, here he was, pouring himself into the basuri, trying to become someone else, trying to transform his heartache into something tangible.

And just as the intensity of his music reached its peak, the door creaked open.

Anay's parents stood there, their eyes wide as they watched the scene unfold. The sight of Anay, alone in the hall, playing with such passion and grief, struck them speechless. The music was breathtaking—a perfect, heart-wrenching storm of sound—but it was the emotions beneath the notes that held them captive.

But it wasn't just the music that caught their attention. As they made their way toward the room, they found Radhika. She had fallen asleep by the window, her head resting against the sill, her body limp with exhaustion. The soft expression on her face, the quiet calm in her sleep—it was as if she had been lulled into some gentle, unreachable dream.

Radhika hadn't realized that she had fallen asleep in the storm, lost in the arms of a dream, with no sense of the man who was playing a symphony of brokenness just a few feet away.

The room was heavy with silence. Anay's parents stood frozen, unsure of what to say or do. The music still echoed in the background, each note a poignant reminder of the young man's heartache.

But no one moved. The storm outside continued its relentless assault, as if the world itself was holding its breath.

XVI
The Illusion of Us

The rain had quieted into a rhythm softer than before, but the air still pulsed with a strange, heavy echo. The smell of wet earth mingled with the delicate, almost sacred scent of sandalwood incense still burning from Radhika's room. The thunder had passed, but it had left a trace behind—in broken silences, in damp hearts.

Anay's parents stood at the entrance, frozen.

His mother's hand was still on the knob of the half-open door, her eyes wide and disbelieving. His father stood beside her, soaked to the knee, umbrella forgotten on the porch.

For a long minute, all they could hear was the flute.

No, not just a flute—a storm grieving through hollow bamboo. A soul unraveling through melody. His fingers had danced over the bansuri like it was a part of him—as if he wasn't playing it, but rather, it was playing him.

And now, they saw the artist.

Anay sat on the edge of the open balcony, his back slightly hunched, soaked in the rain but unaware. Water cascaded from his hair, his kurta clung to his frame. The flute rested loosely in his fingers now, spent. His gaze was lost—not in the sea, not in the city—but somewhere deeper. Somewhere unspeakable.

His mother whispered his name, "Anay…"

He turned slowly, eyes tired—not from sleep, but from feeling too much.

Behind them, the wind still roared, sweeping into the house like it had permission. His father's face was unreadable, caught between awe and concern. But they didn't speak, not yet.

And then, almost in sync, they turned toward the source of the stillness.

Radhika.

She lay curled near the window in her room, fast asleep. The rain hadn't touched her, but it had touched everything around her—her books, her half-written letters, the little flowers kept in a clay bowl by the windowsill. Her lips carried the faintest smile. A dreamer deep in a dream.
She had fallen asleep believing she was in someone's arms.

They didn't wake her.

The house breathed heavily that night.

Later, Anay's mother placed a shawl over Radhika. She lingered, watching her face with motherly affection and quiet worry.

"She looks peaceful," she murmured. "But there's something... something fragile about it."

His father stood beside Anay now. "That was... incredible," he said. "I didn't know you could play like that."

Anay didn't answer. He merely nodded, still lost, eyes flickering from his father to the flute and then back to the window.

"Was that pain, Anay?" his father asked, gently.

"Love," Anay replied.

Then corrected himself, "No. It's... what love becomes when it knows it cannot bloom the way it wishes to. When it learns to sit quietly in a corner and still protect the garden."

His father had no words for that.
Just a hand on his shoulder.

That night, the family sat around the dinner table, barely eating. Radhika had not yet awakened.

The silence was not awkward—but reverent. It wrapped around them like a shared knowing, something sacred that no one dared to interpret out loud.

And finally, when Anay's mother broke the silence, her voice was warm:

"She's very special, Anay."

"I know," he said.

"She loves in a language the world doesn't teach," his father added.

And Anay, quietly, replied, "Then I must unlearn mine."

That night, as he walked to his room, Anay paused once more outside hers.

Through the door slightly ajar, he could see her curled up, her hands resting like petals, the edge of the shawl tucked under her chin.

He smiled—barely.

But not the smile of a man defeated.

The smile of someone who had tasted pain but decided to turn it into poetry.

With the flute in his hand, he walked away—not to sleep, but to practice.

Tomorrow, the notes will begin again.

Not just for music.

But for her.

For love.

For understanding.

For the end that may come, and the grace to greet it.

The house had grown quieter since that stormy night—an unnatural quiet, like a breath being held.

Anay sat near the open window of the living room, the basuri in his lap. The sky outside wore a pale, grey melancholy, drizzling softly as if the clouds, too, were whispering secrets they couldn't hold. Inside, the rhythm of the house had shifted. Something was off. But Anay, in his soft determination, mistook it for change—beautiful, hopeful change.

He raised the basuri to his lips.

The first note, *Sa*, flowed through the air gently, like a leaf brushing against water. His fingers moved with learned grace—*Re, Ga, Ma*—he was getting better. He could feel it. Each breath fed the notes with a kind of ache, yet an ease, as if his soul remembered a language his mind hadn't learned.

From the hallway, Radhika stood still.

Hidden, unnoticed.

Her feet, bare, pressed against the wooden floor, but her eyes—her eyes trembled. The music curled into her ears like a whisper from somewhere else. It was *his* whisper—Madhav's. It wasn't Anay's anymore.

She pressed her hand to her chest.

And she turned away.

She walked back into her room and locked the door. And though the basuri played on, the sound made her chest cave. She felt as if the walls were closing in—each note reminding her that she was losing grip on which world she belonged to. The soft flute wasn't grounding her. It was lifting her out of reality, placing her back into Madhav's world, his arms, his illusions.

She curled into a corner of the bed, rocking slightly, silently. Not because she wanted Madhav to return—but because she was scared he *never left.*

Downstairs, Anay smiled faintly to himself, unaware.

Maybe, just maybe, she was starting to see him in the music. Maybe that shiver in her gaze when she looked at him wasn't fear—but fondness.

"Beta," Anay's mother's voice cut through his thoughts one morning. "She doesn't eat on time anymore."

Anay turned from the balcony, surprised. "She told me she had lunch..."

"She didn't," his father added. "We noticed. Sometimes she skips meals. Sometimes she stands in the garden and talks under her breath."

Anay's smile faltered. "She's... just a bit tired."

His mother looked at him gently, but firmly. "Are you sure the basuri is helping?"

He looked away, lips tightening around the answer he didn't want to hear.

The next evening, he found Radhika sitting silently in the prayer room, staring not at the deities, but the shadow between two lamps, as if trying to read a figure that wasn't there. She didn't even realize he had entered. Her eyes were glassy. Her lips moved slightly.

"Madhav..." she whispered, but too low for Anay to hear.

He knelt beside her, brushing a hand near her shoulder.

She flinched.

Startled.

Not at the touch—but at *him.*

As if she hadn't expected *Anay.*

His heart cracked.

She covered the moment quickly, rising with a faint smile. "You were playing again?"

"Yes..." he said softly. "You heard?"

She nodded.

But her smile was vacant.

And it wasn't joy that reflected in her eyes. It was fear.

That night, Anay stood at the terrace alone.

The basuri in his hand, but he didn't play it.

Because suddenly, he wasn't sure whom he was playing it for anymore.

And somewhere, a quiet storm began to gather—not in the sky, but inside him.

The clouds outside were brooding.

A storm was no longer a metaphor—it was coming alive. Lightning flickered across the walls like fractured truths trying to escape. Inside the house, the silence was thick, almost theatrical. Every breath Anay took felt like standing at the edge of something irreversible.

His parents had just left—reluctant, concerned—but Anay had insisted. "Go," he'd said. "We'll be okay."

But he wasn't okay. Not anymore.

He had loved quietly for years, patiently for seasons, but now, love was screaming inside him. Loud, aching, and desperate. It no longer begged to be felt—it demanded to be seen.

And tonight, it will be heard.

He walked through the hall with purpose, past the window where the basuri rested—his newfound truth. Each step was a rebellion against the silence. He climbed the stairs, one by one, and opened the door to her room.

Radhika sat by the window, talking to someone who wasn't there. Smiling softly into a void. Her silhouette in the fading blue of the evening looked like a painting fading at the edges.

He watched her. And something broke.

"Radhika," he said, quietly.

She turned, startled—eyes flickering like a dream interrupted.

"Come with me," he said. No questions. No warmth.

She followed. Down the stairs, to the center of the house.

There lay the basuri, gleaming faintly as if it knew its moment had come. As if the wood remembered Krishna, remembered centuries of love and longing.

He pointed to the rug.

"Sit," he said.

She sat. Confused. Curious.

Anay stood before her like a man about to bleed. He picked up the basuri—not like an instrument, but like a sword pulled from his chest.

"You want to know what love is, Radhika?" His voice was not soft. It was trembling. Alive. "Then listen."

And he began to play.

It wasn't a tune. It was a rebellion.

Sa... Re... Ga... Ma...—the notes rose, thunder behind them. Not delicate, not sweet—but *hungry*. They tore through the air, clawing at the walls.

Each note screamed:

"I loved you."
"I waited."
"I endured the ghost you chose over me."

His fingers moved not with practice, but with rage, with a grace born from agony. The flute wasn't taught to him—it remembered him. As if in a past life, he had held this very basuri, not as Anay, but as a stormy version of Krishna. A god with no temple. A lover with no Radha.

The breath he blew wasn't just breath—it was the ash of every hope he ever lit for her.

His eyes were shut, but his soul was wide open. Every note vibrated with fury, with grief, with the kind of pain that makes a man dangerous to himself. The storm outside clapped in applause, and lightning carved her name across the sky.

Radhika starred, frozen. The man in front of her wasn't just Anay anymore—he was something else. Something ancient. Something holy. Something on the edge of madness.

And when the final note collapsed into silence...

He lowered the basuri, eyes meeting hers—burning, begging, breaking.

"Well?" he asked, voice hollow. "Am I not enough?"

Radhika's lips parted. A breath. A thousand words unsaid. She swallowed the thunder.

"You play better than Madhav," she said quietly. "You play... with a fire he never had."

His heart jolted.

"But?" he whispered.

She looked down, her voice a dagger wrapped in silk.

"But I still choose him."

Lightning cracked again, this time not outside—but inside him. His chest tightened, the way hearts do when they lose their last war.

"Why?" he asked. "Why?! Why, Radhika?! He's not even *real!*" His voice thundered. "Why are you burning both of us for a dream?!"

She looked up. And for the first time in a long time—her eyes didn't float in the clouds. They were sharp. Real.

"I know," she said.

The storm paused.

"I know he's not real," she continued, voice level, almost serene. "I know he's a part of me. A piece my mind created."

Anay felt his knees tremble. "Then why... why hold onto it?"

She smiled—broken and beautiful.

"Because some lies," she whispered, "feel more like home than any truth ever could."

He fell to his knees in front of her. A man, stripped of all pride.

"I played the basuri for you, Radhika. I gave you every drop of me."

"I know," she said, a tear slipping down her cheek.

"Then why does it still not reach you?"

Her whisper landed like a knife:

"Because my heart doesn't hear this world anymore, Anay. It only hears him."

And there—beneath the crescendo of thunder and heartbreak—ended a chapter not of music, not of madness, but of the kind of love that ruins you forever.

The room was suffocating, heavy with the aftermath of the storm outside. The wind howled, throwing sheets of rain against the window. Inside, the air was thick with a kind of tension, an unsaid truth that had been building for too long.

Anay's hands gripped the basuri, trembling, not with the aftermath of his performance, but with a storm of his own. His eyes locked on Radhika, who sat on the edge of the rug, eyes downcast, as if trying to escape the weight of his gaze. He could feel her shifting—something in her was breaking, but not in the way he'd imagined. Not in the way that would bring her closer to him.

He could feel the ache in his chest, the cold realization settling into his bones. He had poured every ounce of himself into the music, into learning the basuri, into her—only to realize that everything he was giving was never meant for her. Not truly.

"Why, Radhika?" His voice cracked like thunder in the stillness. "Why did you even marry me? Why did you ruin my life so selfishly?" His words were raw, dripping with frustration, pain, and confusion. "Why did you let me love you when you knew your heart would never belong to me?"

Her eyes lifted slowly, meeting him. There was no anger there, no defensiveness. Only understanding. Deep, sorrowful understanding.

She didn't look away. Instead, she spoke softly, her voice breaking but steady.

"Anay, you don't understand," she said, her gaze steady, like she was trying to explain the depth of an ocean to someone who had never touched water. "It's not about you. It never was."

He took a step forward, his hands shaking, as if to reach for something—anything that could give him the answer, but there was nothing.

"What do you mean?" His voice was a whisper, barely audible over the storm. "You're telling me you've known this whole time? That you were living a lie with me, when you already knew that your love was... with him?" The word felt like a curse on his tongue.

She didn't flinch. She was quiet for a moment, collecting her thoughts as the storm outside howled louder.

"No," she said, shaking her head slowly. "It's not about a lie. And it's not about him either." She took a long breath, looking at the floor, trying to find the right words. "It's about love being so different from what we're told it should be."

Anay frowned, his mind racing. "I don't understand. I've done everything. I've loved you like no one else could. I learned the basuri for you, Radhika. Can't you see? I gave everything for you!"

She raised a hand, stopping him, her expression not harsh, but gentle. "I know you did. You learned it because you love me, and that's what makes it so difficult. But love isn't just about learning. It's not just about sacrifices. It's more than that—it's about *faith*. About loyalty. About something you can't touch or see. And that's what I've had for him."

Anay's chest tightened. "Faith? Loyalty? Radhika, he doesn't even exist. He's a part of your mind. A figment of your imagination!" His voice cracked, as if he could barely keep the flood of emotions contained.

She lowered her gaze, her face softening. "And that's where you're wrong, Anay. You see, love isn't a thing you control. You can't make it fit into the mold you think it should. With Madhav... it was never about the physical. It was about something so deep, so ingrained in my soul that no reality, no matter how perfect, could ever replace it. You see, even though I know Madhav isn't real, my love for him... it transcends anything I could have with anyone else."

Anay's heart broke at her words, but he had to know. "But why did you marry me then? If you knew this all along, why did you let me live this lie?"

She inhaled slowly, her voice shaking but steady. "Because I didn't want to hurt you, Anay. I thought I could do this for you, for your love—for the love you gave me. I thought I could love you in the way you wanted. But the truth is, I couldn't. Not fully. Not the way I loved him. And that's not your fault. It's just the way love works."

He clenched his fists, his breath ragged, struggling to keep his composure. "But if your love for him is so deep, then why choose me at all? Why let me love you when your heart already belongs to someone who doesn't exist?" His words came out sharp and raw.

Her eyes filled with unshed tears, but she was resolute. "Because love doesn't have boundaries. You taught me that, Anay. You loved me in a way that I never knew I could be loved. But my loyalty... My love for Madhav isn't bound by anything. Even if he's not real, he *is* to me. He's my truth."

The silence between them grew heavy, but Anay wasn't finished. He had one last question, the one that had been gnawing at him for so long—the one that had haunted him since the first time he'd picked up the basuri.

"Then... how did you create him, Radhika?" His voice was barely a whisper now. "How did you create this... this *Madhav*? And why did you let me believe in him? If you're so aware of your condition... Why, Radhika? Why?"

She looked at him then, her face pale, the truth weighing heavily on her chest. "You want to know how he was created, Anay? I didn't create him," she whispered. "He was always there. Just like you were. He was always a part of me... always waiting for the right moment to come alive."

Her voice dropped even lower, almost to a whisper. "He was a fragment of something I didn't understand... something I never could. He is my Krishna, Anay. My Madhav. And I, his Radha."

Anay's heart stopped. His breath caught in his throat.

He understood then.

Radhika had never been just *his*. And Madhav had never just been a figment of her imagination.

It was a love that transcended everything.

XVII
THE DIVINE COLLAPSE

The house stood still—too still. Even the ceiling fan made no sound, as if it too had been silenced by the confrontation that had just passed. It wasn't just a pause in words between Anay and Radhika; it was the kind of silence that pressed against the chest, where breaths feel heavier than they should, and glances are avoided like sharp knives.

They no longer shared meals in the same room. Anay would leave his cup of tea untouched. Radhika, once floating in her dreams, now floated in the guilt of waking up to them. The echoes of their last conversation still lingered—Anay's trembling voice asking *why she married him*... Radhika's tearful clarity that love, in its truest form, does not ask to be returned.

But silence wasn't still. It shifted shapes in the air between them. It hovered over unfinished books, echoed through the walls that once held laughter. Even the basuri, which Anay had kept carefully wrapped in a velvet cloth, seemed to hold its breath.

Radhika now kept mostly to herself. She would stare into nothingness longer than usual, her fingers tracing invisible patterns on her lap, sometimes humming unknown melodies—ones that perhaps only Madhav knew. She was physically present, yet every minute she looked more and more like a memory.

Anay watched her from a distance. No longer with the gaze of a lover hoping for reciprocation, but of a man standing at the edge of a shore watching someone he loves sail toward a storm he cannot save them from. His fingers often itched to hold the basuri again, but not for display, not for love—but for surrender. He had learned the notes, now he needed to unlearn everything else.

And then came the sky.

That morning, the clouds over the city hung low and heavy, as if something monumental waited to break through. Somewhere in the lanes of their neighborhood, conch shells blew and drums began to thump. The annual *Dahi Handi* festival has arrived again. This time, the celebration didn't knock. It barged in.

Modern day, the scene begins with the Dahi Handi festival, but this time, everything feels different. Anay stands in the midst of the chaos, but the vibrant, loud festival seems to slow down around him. The music fades into a distant hum. The world feels as though it is moving in slow motion.

Radhika climbs the human pyramid, her movements graceful yet uncertain, much like the way she's lived her life—always reaching for something higher, something unattainable. Her eyes meet Anay's briefly, and in that fleeting glance, something unspoken passes between them. His heart skips a beat, and for a moment, time stops completely. Her foot slips.

It's like watching it all in slow motion: the way her body tilts, the way her arms flail as she loses her grip, and the way her face expresses an innocent surprise—like a flower just beginning to fall from its stem. The crowd's voices blur into the background, and Anay watches in silence. This is the same fall, the same helplessness, but now, it feels like the fall of her soul—her constant struggle with the unattainable.

But this time, it's different. He doesn't rush to catch her. He doesn't feel the urgency that he once did. Instead, he stands still, watching her fall, and his heart aches in a quiet, almost painful way. The memory of her fall—when he first saw her, when his heart first recognized her as someone to protect, as someone to love—now comes crashing back, not with hope, but with the weight of understanding

Before he can fully comprehend the weight of the moment, Kabir's voice rips through the tension, shattering the silence.

"Anay," Kabir's voice is curious, almost too eager, breaking the fragile stillness. "I've been meaning to ask... How did she even *create* him?"

The words hit Anay like a splash of cold water. His gaze shifts to Kabir, but his thoughts are still lost in the slow-motion images of Radhika's fall, and now this—this question that somehow pulls him out of his own pain and into something sharper, more immediate.

He looks at Kabir, still lost in the thought of Radhika, but Kabir's relentless questioning brings him back to the surface.

"How did she create him?" Kabir repeats, his voice edged with both confusion and curiosity. "Madhav, I mean. Was it... was it something inside her mind?"

The question lingers between them, suspended in the air, heavy and demanding. Anay looks at Kabir, and for a moment, there's no answer. There's only the pounding in his chest, the ache of an unspoken truth.

Finally, Anay speaks, his voice low, almost pained, as if the words themselves are too much to carry.

"She... she read about Radha and Krishna," Anay begins, each word slow and deliberate, as if he's been carrying this weight for a lifetime. "She read about them, again and again, until the idea of Krishna... the love of Radha for him... became her refuge. Her comfort. She didn't create Madhav, Kabir. She created him because she needed him. She needed someone to hold her in the same way Radha was held by Krishna—someone who would never let her fall, even when she couldn't fully reach him."

He pauses, and his voice tightens, as if the words are too painful to speak.

"Radha... She was always close to Krishna, always longing, but never able to fully embrace him. And that... that same ache... is what Radhika felt. She needed Madhav, not just for love, but to fill that unspoken space. That ache. But she never wanted him as I wanted her. She never wanted to be mine. Not really."

Anay's gaze drifts, his eyes distant. His breath is slow, measured. The weight of his own words hangs heavy in the air, and for a moment, it feels like the ground beneath him has shifted, like the world has tilted slightly.

Kabir stands still, the gravity of Anay's words settling over him. He opens his mouth, but no words come out. The realization dawns slowly—Anay has just peeled back the layers of the woman they both know, revealing something deeper, something that was always there, hidden behind the veil of normalcy.

Anay takes a deep breath. "I am not Krishna, Kabir. And I am not Madhav. I am just a man who tried... who tried to love her, to be the one who would catch her. But in the end, I was never meant to. Not the way she needed me to be."

Kabir stands, quiet, unsure of what to say. But the question lingers, echoing in the silence.

Then... Then who were you Anay?

Anay looks at Kabir one last time, his voice barely above a whisper, as if he's speaking to himself more than anyone else.

"I was never the one, Kabir. I was always just... Ayan. The man who tried to love Radha, but never could."

The scene was set in a flurry of color, sound, and light. The air crackled with the anticipation of the Dahi Handi festival. The crowd was a kaleidoscope of faces, each person's eyes fixed on the human pyramid climbing higher toward the prize above—the pot filled with curd. But above them, in the center of it all, stood Radhika, poised and fragile as if the weight of the world rested solely upon her delicate frame.

The moment stretched into infinity.

Her breath was steady, her pulse racing, but inside, everything felt oddly still. As she stood, balanced upon the shoulders of those beneath her, her heart beat in quiet rhythm with the crowd's collective excitement. The world around her seemed to blur. She felt the sway, the gentle rocking beneath her, the shifting weight. Her legs, trembling slightly, were kept steady by an invisible force. There was a strange quietness within her—an emptiness that pulled her closer to something she could not name, could not touch, but knew existed.

Her fingers, reaching for the pot above, grazed the air with a silent prayer, as if in that very moment she could pull down the heavens themselves. The cheers of the crowd surged, their voices blending into one ecstatic roar, but Radhika felt herself slipping away from it all. She could feel herself falling, but this time, it wasn't terrifying. It was *liberating.*

Her heart didn't race with fear; it quickened with a strange peace, as though her body already knew what was coming.

The fall wasn't an accident. It was inevitable.

In that moment, everything around her seemed to slow, the world blurring like a watercolor painting. The sky dimmed as if the sun had suddenly withdrawn from the scene, leaving the world drenched in soft shadows. The sound of the crowd became muffled, almost surreal, as if the universe had wrapped her in a cocoon of stillness.

She could feel the others—beneath her—losing their grip. The pyramid began to falter, and in slow motion, she felt herself tumbling. She didn't scream. She didn't flinch. Instead, she exhaled softly, her chest rising and falling as if releasing the burden she had carried for so long. The fall wasn't about physical pain—it was about the release of something far deeper. A letting go of all the weight of expectation. The weight of love that couldn't be returned.

I'm falling... but I am at peace.

Her body spiraled downward, and time seemed to stretch. Her gaze was fixed on the sky above, watching as the light shifted from warm gold to cold silver. Her hands flailed in the air as if reaching for something that would never be there. But there was no panic, no desperation. Only an odd contentment—like someone who had known this moment all along.

She was falling toward the ground, but in her heart, she was already in the arms of *Madhav*. He was there, as real to her as the air she breathed, cradling her, soothing her. Even in the fall, there was a strange comfort. *Madhav...* She felt him there, his presence enveloping her like the breath she took, like the world itself.

As her body neared the earth, the sensation of time dilating intensified. Everything around her became a haze of colors and sounds, indistinguishable and irrelevant. There was nothing now but the quiet beat of her heart, and the unspoken promise of love that she had always known, always *felt*. The moment was sacred. It was the culmination of everything—of all her struggles, her confusion, and her acceptance. She *was* falling, but she was also *rising*. Rising in the knowledge that in her heart, she was always with him.

And then, just as her body was about to make contact with the earth, something shifted in the air. A sudden gust of wind, sharp and cold, wrapped around her. The ground beneath her seemed to blur into a swirling mess, and she saw something—a flash of color—a hint of blue and green, catching the light, swirling in the air with a quiet grace.

A peacock feather.

It fluttered down slowly, as though it had been waiting for this moment. The feather seemed to descend with a kind of divine purpose, untouched by gravity, carried on the winds of fate. Its beauty was unparalleled, as it glinted in the dimming light.

Radhika felt the wind catch the feather and bring it to her cheek. It touched her skin gently, almost lovingly, like a kiss from the divine.

The feather stayed there for a moment—soft, light, and yet incredibly significant. She didn't need to look at it to know its meaning. It was a message from the heavens—an acknowledgment of her love, of the devotion that transcended time and space.

Her hand rose to touch the feather, feeling the coolness of it against her skin. It was as if the universe had reached out to her, acknowledging her truth. Her love for Madhav was unlike any love the world had ever known. It wasn't bound by time, space, or flesh. It was spiritual. It was eternal.

This is my love... the love of Radha, the love of Krishna, the love that cannot be explained...

Her eyes closed, and she felt peace, an all-encompassing peace. Her love was different from what the world told her it should be. She could never be the ideal wife, the perfect partner to someone who loved her with all his heart. She could never be what Anay wanted her to be.

But she had already given her heart, not to a man, but to an idea—*Madhav.* A love so pure, so impossible, that it couldn't be bound by the expectations of the world.

She knew she couldn't return to the world below, to the life she had before. She could never go back to the mundane. Her love, her soul, was free now. Free to love in a way that couldn't be defined by society.

And as the feather remained against her cheek, Radhika smiled softly. The world around her could never understand, never know the depth of what she had. But in her heart, she knew it didn't matter.

Her love was eternal. And that was enough.

ABOUT THE AUTHOR

Arnav Herlekar is a writer whose work delves into the intricate landscapes of love, identity, and the profound emotions that often go unspoken. His debut novel, *Little Things*, captivated readers with its exploration of the small, yet significant moments that shape our lives and relationships. With his second novel, *Forbidden Love of the Old Book*, Arnav continues his exploration of the human heart, focusing on the quiet ache of unrequited love and the complexity of self-discovery.

Arnav's writing is marked by a poetic style, where every word is chosen to evoke deep emotional resonance. He is fascinated by the spaces between words—the moments of silence that carry as much weight as the loudest declarations. His characters often navigate the delicate dance between vulnerability and strength, and his stories are a celebration of the quiet, enduring power of love.

Outside of writing, Arnav enjoys reflecting on life's subtleties, finding inspiration in the world around him—whether it's a fleeting moment, a song, or an unspoken connection. His work invites readers to pause, think, and feel deeply, as he believes that the most important stories are often the ones told in the quietest of voices.